THE
ARTIST'S
WIDOW

A NOVEL

THE

ARTIST'S

WIDOW

A NOVEL

by Shena Mackay

MOYER BELL
Wakefield, Rhode Island & London

Published by Moyer Bell

First Edition

LIBRARY OF CONGRESS
CATALOGING-IN-PUBLICATION DATA

Mackay, Shena.
    The artist's widow / Shena Mackay.
— 1st ed.

    p.   cm.
    I. Title
    PR6063.A2425A89   1999
    823'.914—dc21   98-41720
    ISBN 1-55921-229-2 (cloth)   CIP

Printed in the United States of America
on elemental chlorine and acid free
recycled paper with soy based ink.
Distributed in North America by
Publishers Group West, 1700 4th St.,
Berkeley, CA 94710. 800-788-3123
(in California 510-528-1444)

For Henry Gabriel Smith
and Daisy Morag Smith

THE
ARTIST'S
WIDOW

A NOVEL

CHAPTER ONE

Every artist leaves behind a shadowy retrospective exhibition of the pictures that were never painted. Although perhaps only one of the guests at the private view sensed their presence, the spaces between the canvases on the walls were swarming with the ghosts of ideas and thwarted images. It was the sort of party that John and Lyris Crane hated. Louis Viner Fine Art was a Mayfair gallery that stretched through a long white rectangle which amplified the noise, with a bottleneck in the doorway where people checking their coats and reaching for the champagne that greeted them met smokers fighting their way out to stand in the drizzle. The hot August weather had broken that afternoon.

Lyris was there on her own. In one hand she held a glass with a purple sediment and in the other the bunch of flowers which someone had brought her from his garden. Louis had draped his arm across her shoulders in a proprietorial yet patronizing way, trapping her and reminding her of a snake that a man had slung round her neck once in Tangiers. As he spoke he puffed gusts of wine into her face. Now and then she glimpsed a waitress circulating with a bottle but it was always empty before it reached their corner.

Lyris glanced at her watch, and saw that the flowers were scattering tiny black dots, seeds or insects, over the front of her pale dress. John had the perfect excuse for being late tonight for he was unavoidably and indefinitely detained at Golders Green. This was the Private View of John Crane, 1918–1996: The Last Paintings. Lyris felt a pang of envy for John, among the flowers and berries of the crematorium gardens. But the trees would be gathering darkness now, the reeds and bulrushes whispering, a chilly dew rising to meet the rain. Time to come indoors.

A young man with a round orange-stubbled head and a fringe of orange moustache clapped Louis on the shoulder. His eyelids, with a bristle of pale lashes, were tender and his eyes dull green and hard.

"Louis, my man! Who do you have to screw to get a drink in this place? You're going to have to sack your caterers, you know."

"Lyris, have you met Nathan Pursey?" Louis asked, removing his arm at last.

"Nathan's my great nephew. By marriage. Hello Nathan, how nice of you to come. Nathan's one of the Purley Purseys," she added in explanation, or apology.

Nathan had the pointed Pursey nose, which pulled up the lip like a rodent's to expose the front teeth, with a depression above one nostril where a stud had been removed. His teeth were strong and white, whereas in some of the clan they were as yellow as a beaver's. He had met Louis at a show at the Serpentine Gallery and had made it his business to cultivate him.

"Cheers, great auntie by marriage. Well, I see they've all come out of the woodwork tonight."

Nathan was wearing a white shirt clotted with pigments over chef's trousers, and a burned-out roll-up was stuck behind his ear. Three champagne glasses dangled by their stems between his fingers. He raked his eyes round the gallery, taking in Savile Row tailoring and label jeans, a tuxedo with a glittering AIDS emblem, peacock blue silk, all the lustre and glitter, the stained velvet and mothy grandeur of ancient *haute bohème,* and the bare shoulders of girls. Lyris could see that he wanted it all for himself. She remembered him as a little boy at a family party loading his paper plate with cocktail sausages, chocolate fingers, gherkins, cake and crisps until it collapsed, and with white powder on his nose at her husband's funeral.

"You're living in North London now, aren't you, Nathan?" she asked.

"Yes, Why?"

"I thought so."

His customary smell of cannabis, mildew and Marlboros had acquired top notes of hummus and stale white wine. It was true that it was a surprisingly impressive turnout. She hoped that there was a rash of scarlet dots on the paintings that nobody could see.

"It's funny," said Nathan. "I was just going to lig my way in, as you do, when it struck me that Uncle John would definitely have wanted me to be here tonight. Guess my invite must have got lost in the post. Well, better go and mingle I suppose. Work the room as they say. By the way, Lyris, did you catch that feature on me and my mates in the *Sunday Times?* What a laugh. We were all totally bladdered."

Lyris shook her head.

"Get Mum to send you a copy. Apparently she bought up the newsagent's. You saw it, didn't you, Louis? Yep, me and the lads are really putting Tufnell Park on the map."

"Isn't it still *on* the Northern Line now, then? It always used to be," said Lyris.

Nathan backed away to look for somebody to impress. Louis watched him dump his empty glasses on a passing tray, snatch a bottle of red wine and push his way into a circle of writers and painters who didn't pause in their conversation. Nathan took a glug from the bottle and picked at a clot on the front of his shirt. It was not, as Lyris supposed, paint. He was furious that he had not been invited and scowled round the room, thinking he recognized various people from the funeral, some with babies strapped to their chests. Nathan's interest in babies was limited to dismembered plastic dolls. No doubt they'd all be troughing at the Ivy later while he was plonking home on the Northern Line. The old bat had really dissed him this time. Nathan belched and, catching sight of a gorgeous bird wasting herself on some wizened scrote, began to move in on her.

"He'll go far, that nephew of yours," Louis remarked. "One of the movers and shakers *sans doute*. You must be thrilled. He was a protégé of John's, wasn't he? I've promised to make a studio visit soon."

"That boy couldn't draw his way out of a paper bag. Never could and never will. He was the only child I've ever known who couldn't do magic painting books. Yes, I'm sure Nathan *will* go far."

A pond with green scum on its surface came into her mind. And yet she was fond of the boy because she had known him as a baby, a Mabel Lucie Attwell elf. She sighed for him; so young, and yet so *passé*, and with an incipient beer belly. Against his better judgment John had pulled strings to get Nathan into Chelsea and now here was Louis, John's dealer, apparently eager to exhibit Nathan's self-indulgently assembled detritus. Nathan had treated Chelsea like an extension of school, mucking about and bunking off lectures. They had given him his degree though. Nathan and his pals had even colonized the Colony Room, unaware that their custom had destroyed any tattered remnants of its glamor.

"Louis dear, do you see that couple jammed into the corner?" she said.

"Who let *them* in?"

"Could you go and be nice to them please? They're very good friends and neighbors. I tried to introduce them as soon as they arrived. Their portraits are hanging over there."

"Ah. Of course they are."

"John was very fond of them. Before you ask them what they do, Tony has a washing machine repair business and Anne's a dinner lady at our local school."

Louis made a derisively submissive little bow and left her as Clovis Ingram came up and kissed her hand. He was a tall olive-skinned man in his late forties, wearing a brown shirt with a turquoise tie, who always reminded Lyris of a Burmese cat, and not only because she once had a chocolate Burmese called Clovis. Lyris had known his father who had had a framemaker's business in Maida Vale, which Clovis on inheriting the premises had converted to Criterion Books.

Clovis had arrived early and spent some time looking at the paintings. There were those who dismissed them as the daubs of a lost old man sploshing away like a child in a waterproof smock at nursery school, others praised the liberation of the loose brushstrokes and swirls. The last canvases burned with the brilliant chemical derangement of autumn when the slow fuses smouldering up the stalks of senescent leaves burst into mineral fire.

"Lyris, you're looking wonderful. Like a drawing in chalks— of white and mauve irises. Can I get you a drink?"

"Thank you. No thank you. But I do feel rather chalky. I don't like standing for very long and these ridiculous shoes are killing me. I keep hoping that John will arrive to rescue me so that we can go home and have a quiet supper in front of the telly."

Clovis looked at her long, narrow feet without speaking. To be pushing eighty and to have come to a party in blue suede shoes was deserving of more admiration than he could express. The toes were almond-shaped, pale blue fuzzy buds. Eventually he said, "I'll find you a chair. There must be one downstairs."

"Please don't. I'd be trapped like a dowager with some kindly *ingénue* feeling duty-bound to crouch at my knee and then be unable to get up from embarrassment."

"I'm leaving in a minute. Do you want to come with me? We could have a bite to eat, or I'll put you in a taxi— *Who* is that amazing girl with your appalling nephew? She looks like Nefertiti. Is she the girlfriend?"

"I've no idea. The last time I saw him was at John's funeral and he was with a different girl. A Rastafarian, I think. It's all a bit of a blur. You must have met her. I understood that they were what's called an item. No, Clovis, thank you. Louis is taking me to supper and it would be rather impolite to leave. On the other hand, he's just been extremely rude about two very dear friends . . . perhaps I will."

But Clovis was no longer listening, he had just seen a gauzy mass of agate-colored hair; Isobel his former wife raised her glass to him in an ironic toast. He stepped back from the people converging on Lyris with a sheaf of bronze lilies in copper beech leaves. It seemed to Lyris that the room had become much noisier, like a cave filled with the roar of the sea. She felt dizzy and shook her head to clear it, smiling at Clovis who was leaving without her, and tried to concentrate on the voices that were swimming around her. She must pull herself together for John's sake. Put on a good show. It was no use. She couldn't make out what anybody was saying, and she knew that she would have to stand there like a deaf white cat, purring lest she should offend.

Clovis might have shared Lyris's brief sea fantasy; one of his private names for Isobel when they were still married had been The Wounded Squid because she was so clinging and so easily hurt into squirting her purple sentimental ink over everything. The map of the world was stained with her compassion. Of course he had found it charming in her once. Izzie had a gift for making you feel you had betrayed her on occasions when you hadn't; her neck was permanently bowed by an invisible tray of flags for some cause of which you were too crass to be aware. Clovis and Izzie had a daughter, Miranda, who was fifteen, and who was on holiday in France.

From the corner of his eye he saw a tentacle shoot out and engulf a canapé from a salver which had eluded him. As he shouldered his way through, Clovis passed Nefertiti looking bored in a white shift and heaps of gold and turquoise jewelery. Nathan had captured a venerable painter by the tassels of his white silk scarf.

"Jacob, my man! Just the bloke I'm looking for! I need to pick your brains for an installation I'm doing. You know that *Kristallnacht* thingy in Berlin where the Nazis smashed all the glass in the shop windows?"

While Clovis waited to collect his coat he heard the man in front of him say to his wife,

"If I'd had to listen to one more of those condescending prats telling me how they'd been ripped off by their washing machine repair men . . ."

"I still think we should have said goodbye to Lyris."

"No chance in that crush. Anyway, you can see her tomorrow."

Clovis watched them help each other into their raincoats and then negotiate the knots of smokers blocking the doorway. Outside, the woman put up her umbrella and put it down again and the man lit a cigarette.

"Tony, do you think we were supposed to have given that girl a tip, the one that gave us our coats? Only she looked so snooty . . ."

"Don't worry about it, we won't be seeing her again."

"Excuse me," Clovis said, recognizing them, "I think we met at John's funeral. I'd have known you from your portraits of course. Look good, don't they?"

Behind them came the crash of a glass that somebody would try to blame somebody else for breaking, the mouths talked on and in the lavatory hot soapy water splashed on to the bronze lilies which a solicitous assistant had placed in the hand basin.

Lyris, home at last, ran a sinkful of water for her battered flowers and kicked off her shoes. The pale blue was streaked with black marks and the front of the left shoe bore the imprint of a man's heavy sole. She would never wear them again, just as she imagined she would not see Louis again. She had spent the taxi ride home in a state of disbelief at the humiliations that had been heaped on her and angry with herself for accepting them. It was because she was grateful to Louis for arranging the show. He had taken over the gallery from his mother who had been John's dealer for forty years and had never made much money from or for him.

It transpired that Louis had not booked a restaurant. "Has Nathan left?" he had asked, looking disappointed. As Lyris hobbled along keeping pace with him and the bunch of people he had accrued, she tried to tell herself that she was having an anxiety dream from which she would soon wake. They ended up in a Thai restaurant where the service was so slow that several bottles of wine had been drunk before the food came. Green chili seared her tongue and she sipped mineral water miserably to cool her mouth and surreptitiously wash out the burning seed trapped at the top of a tooth. A long tooth. Nathan had depressed her deeply and her flowers, so kindly intended and such a blasted nuisance, were bundled under the table where some lost their heads. There had been no suggestion that she was the guest of honor or that she should not contribute to the inevitably disputed bill for food she had not eaten and wine she had not drunk.

Eventually, they were out on the pavement again. When a taxi approached, Louis leaped into the road. As Lyris grabbed the door handle and climbed in she saw a look of surprise on Louis's face which suggested that he had hailed it for himself. All in all, if she counted the shoes, the evening had cost her the best part of a hundred pounds.

She went into the studio. An unfinished canvas stood on the easel. She put on a record, Ella singing "This Time The Dream's On Me," unscrewed the cap of a tube of paint, squeezed out a bead of ultramarine and took a brush from a jar.

CHAPTER TWO

Clovis had intended to take a taxi home to Maida Vale but none passed him as he walked along Dover Street and turned into Piccadilly and he found himself heading for Green Park station. The Lees had offered to drop him off somewhere in their van but they were going south. A few wet leaves blown from the park followed him down the entrance to the tube. A busker was packing up his flute and cap.

At eight o'clock few people were traveling and Clovis found himself alone on the escalator, struck by the strangeness of his solitude as he was carried down the empty conveyor belt. Then he heard feet thudding, running from one of the platforms. There was a dull crash, and silence, except for the mechanical whine. The pitch of the escalator was so steep that he could see nothing below him but, alarmed, he peered across the black moving handrail, over the central staircase, to the up escalator. A person, fair head pointing downwards, one boot scrabbling feebly to get a purchase on the step above as he lay on the stairs, was borne upside down past him, inexorably up the silver slope.

Clovis stood transfixed as the distance between them was stretched. He jumped the last few steps and still he stood, watching the diminishing twitching figure curled on its side. He looked for the alarm. There, red in its silver diamond-shaped case. Should he? The fallen one was out of sight now, must be nearing the top. Shout for help? Dry-mouthed, Clovis turned away, tensed against screams and screeching metal, and walked on to the platform, sick at the thought of a bootlace caught in the disappearing step, metal grinding flesh and bone. But no screams came.

The indicator showed a train due in one minute. Clovis returned to the base of the escalators. The one going up had been switched off. It loomed motionless. All his blood seemed to drain into his shoes. He turned back and became aware of a couple of people on the platform and heard the approaching train. There was a swirling in his head like debris drifting in the aftermath of an explosion. He almost stepped off the edge as the train drew in, but saw the face of the driver at the controls and let it pass. When the train stopped he got in and sat down. As the doors' rubber lips closed, sealing him in, he thought, "That's it. I am damned. Now I have put myself beyond the pale for ever. I am going to pay for this."

The substantial creamy houses of Maida Vale were glazed with the recent rain that had washed swirls and eddies of grit and twiggy green leaves over the pavement. As Clovis walked from Warwick Avenue all he saw was the grey rubber kiss of the closing train doors. He shuddered as his shoe pulped a bunch of unripe rowan berries. The light was on in the kitchen of Candy's flat above Criterion Cleaners, silhouetting the jumble of plants and plastic bottles on her windowsill. Clovis could hear the faint yapping of dogs as he hurried with his head bowed in case she should look out. Yet Candy was probably the only person he could have told. He walked on past his own bookshop towards the luminous duck-egg blue globes on either side of the entrance to the mansion block named Criterion Court.

CHAPTER THREE

Nathan woke in his room in the Tufnell Park house to an unpleasant smell. He sniffed his shirt and pulled it over his head, losing a couple of buttons, and lay back trying to remember at which point he had lost the girl. He could recall the two of them drinking on the pavement outside a pub. Had he taken her to the Colony? He supposed he would have because she looked like she could have been a supermodel if she'd wanted. Then at some point she must have dumped him. He couldn't even remember her name.

Nathan reached painfully to the floor for a can with a dribble of lager left, forgetting that he had used it as an ashtray. He gagged on a flashback of himself sobbing over a payphone to his old girlfriend Jackee Wigram. I must've dreamt it, he thought, I'd never sink to that, not when I can pull class like—whats'ername. He retrieved the fact that she was half Egyptian. It was Nathan's boast that he'd always had a taste for dark meat, in women as much as in the Christmas turkey; which was one of the reasons why that wigga Jackee had had to go. Her rice 'n' peas was good though. A plastic blow-up of the figure in Munch's *The Cry* was propped in a corner with a half-smoked cigarette in its mouth. Nathan pulled out the cigarette and the screamer gave a little gasp and wobble and began to deflate slowly. Prominent among the magazine pictures and newspaper cuttings stuck to the wall was a large color photograph of the artist Damien Hirst. It was pocked with holes and a dart quivered from the tip of the nose.

Nathan padded in his socks to the shared kitchen, switched on the kettle and went into the bathroom. The mirror showed that a crop of spots like tiny toadstools in sparse orange grass had sprung up overnight in his moustache and the darker bristles on his chin and his eyes were a bit gummed-up. Unmistakably the face of a party animal on the morning after. Some months ago a small photo of the Group had appeared in *ES* Magazine's "Circuit" feature with the caption "Party Animals" and the following week the *Standard's* art critic had rubbished their show in a brief round-up of new galleries. It was the accolade. He tossed the cigarette butt into the loo and aimed at it before standing in the bath to shower. Somebody had stuck a notice to the cistern saying "Please Flush After Use" but already the Sellotape was curling in the steam. He could hear the phone ringing through the noise of the water. Nobody answered it. Perhaps no one else was in. There was a towel among the girlie things on the washing line strung across the window. Nathan used it and threw it back and ate a bit of toothpaste from a tube that had been left on the basin.

The phone was still ringing. He went down to the hall and picked it up. "Nathan? Thank goodness. Are you all right? I've been ringing and ringing. You got me so worried last night when you called I didn't get a wink of sleep. Nathan?"

Nathan dropped the receiver to the floor and went back to the kitchen and switched the kettle on again. He opened the cupboard and surveyed the shelf allocated to Ramesh, the bloke who had just moved in. There was an almost full jar of coffee and a large box of teabags as well as packets and tins and herbs and spices. What a tosser. He'd learn.

It was a short walk to his studio which was a partitioned space in what had once been a garment factory. The top floor of the building was derelict, colonized by pigeons and buddleia sprouting through burned-out windows. Two women machinists had died in the fire, trapped by a locked door. Seb, who occupied the space adjoining Nathan's, had made a series of photo-montages, framed with scorched and melted buttons, based on the tragedy. Nathan stuck his head round Seb's partition.

"What's that horrible pong in here? It smells like something died."

"You tell me. It's coming from your studio. You look a bit rough this morning, my man. Good night out, was it?"

"You could say that." Nathan yawned, scratching his stubble. "I met this woman at a private view and—"

"What private view was that then? You never told anybody."

"Oh, it was at some poncey gallery in Mayfair. Invitation only."

"So?"

"So you weren't invited."

"Since when has that made any difference?"

"Only I *was*. Geezer whose show it was was my uncle. John Crane? Everybody was there. I mean, if a bomb had dropped on that party, bye-bye English art establishment."

Seb glowered under the single black eyebrow on his narrow forehead. His hair, sticking out in greasy feathers, reminded Nathan of a gannet caught in the spillage from an oil-tanker.

"So who did you actually talk to then?"

"You name it. Dealers, artists, loads of people. And I pulled this fantastic Egyptian bird. Fatima."

"Fatima! Did she have her javelin with her?" Seb jeered.

"As it happens, she didn't need it," Nathan smirked, "but we're not talking Fatima Olympic athlete here, my son, we're talking Fatima Queen of the Nile."

"Fatima's not even an Egyptian name. It's Turkish or Cypriot."

"Well she ought to know, I suppose."

"So when are you seeing her again?"

"Later on, as it goes. We're doing lunch."

"So you just dropped by to gloat, is that it? Well don't let me keep you. It's half twelve already."

"She'll wait. These middle-eastern birds know their place."

As Nathan went into his own space Seb called after him.

"I thought we were supposed to be a group. Sharing our contacts and everything. I thought that was supposed to be the point."

A cloud of bluebottles was buzzing round the tub of viscera that formed the base of Nathan's *Dresden* sculpture, setting in motion the mobile of balsawood aeroplanes.

"You little beauties," said Nathan, but the stench was so overpowering that he had to throw the whole installation out of the window. He flicked the switch of the fairylights looping the perspex box that housed a styrofoam head he had begged from the hairdresser's and topped with one of those cotton-wool trimmed Santa hats that loonies wear all the year round. He had taken it from a vagrant sleeping in the doorway, leaving half a sandwich as payment. One of the bulbs must have blown but the dead fairylights only added to the wit of the visual pun. It had been designed to give the finger to certain people who had called his degree show old hat.

He wished he had thought of a better name than Fatima, and as he was supposed to be meeting her for lunch, he would have to go back to the house now, and make out later that he had given her the elbow. Seb's mean little face all contorted with jealousy gave him pleasure though; usually the boot was on the other foot because Seb had a nasty habit of coming up with Nathan's ideas first. Those buttons from the factory fire were a prime example, making Nathan's *Who's Sari Now?* collage look like a rip-off. Still, he thought, the advantages of being a group, in terms of media attention, outweighed the hassles. There were six of them now, all blokes. It was Mitchell who had announced to the lads the seventh member's defection a while ago when they were sitting outside their local, the White Bear. His face was red, under hair pulled back from a center parting into a lank ponytail.

"That fat slag Sophie's only got a one-man show at the Eagle Gallery."

"The treacherous cow!" Nathan spluttered beer over the table.

"Die, bitch!" said Josh.

"Soph's not really that fat, though, is she?" put in Howard who had been hopelessly in love with Sophie for years. His degree show had been a video of Sophie eating lunch. "Slag, definitely. I wouldn't argue with that," he added with the haste of someone who feared he was something of an outsider. He was slender, with light curls already receding over a prominent forehead.

"Well she's out of the Group now, that's for sure. We're better off without her. Boy Bandz, eh? Except for the Spice Girlies—and they're all hype. They won't last five minutes," said Larry, blowing up a crisp packet and exploding it with a black fingernail. Everybody knew his girlfriend had just fired him for a trainee manager at Boots.

"Why don't we go and trash Sophie's private view?" Nathan suggested, but in the event nobody had the energy. By that time they were preparing for their show at the North Pole Gallery off Tufnell Park Road.

The rumor that Charles Saatchi had bought one of Sophie's paintings and was going to show it in the Royal Academy's *Sensation* exhibition of Young British Art had brought Nathan fresh bitterness. Despite the publicity the North Pole show had attracted, Nathan Pursey would not be among the YBAs representing their generation. Even though *Time Out* had singled out his *Dead Sheep* to illustrate its review. That had been a bit of serendipity, tripping over one of those solidified sacks of cement you find outside houses that somebody has started to renovate and given up on. A sack of cement that looked like a dead sheep. His only consolation was that none of the Group had been selected for *Sensation*, but his dad was right; it's not what you know, it's who you know.

Nathan had put this to the Group when they had gathered in Howard's room to hammer out a manifesto for the future. It was late morning and they sat around eating Kentucky fried chicken while they waited for Josh. Nathan was stretched out on Howard's neat bed, shagged out, he told them, after a night on the tiles. He did not explain that he had spent the previous evening at home in Purley, helping his dad redecorate the bathroom, and had caught a train back that morning. By the time Josh sauntered in, lounging in the doorway like a tall dissolute blond schoolboy in a rugby shirt with the sleeves ripped out, all that was left was a box of greasy bones and skin.

"What's the story, morning glory?" he said.

"You look like I feel," said Nathan. "What a night." He stretched luxuriously.

"Yeah, well, if some members of this group showed a bit more commitment to their work instead of clubbing it and chasing after women . . ." said Seb.

Josh reached for Larry's bottle of mineral water and poured it down his throat.

"Thanks, I was parched. Don't suppose anyone can lend us a bit of blow?"

"In your dreams," said Seb.

"To get back to the meeting," Howard said. "What we're up against is the New Establishment, isn't it? Who needs it anyway? The true artist has always got to be an outsider."

He put on his tape of Don McLean singing "Vincent."

"Very funky, Howard," said Mitchell, examining a blister on

the bare heel in his loafer. "What we need is to come up with something so outrageous . . . 'The Shock of the New . . .'"

"How about 'The Shock of the Nearly New?' A faulty electric blanket from a charity shop that electrocutes the spectators?" Josh suggested before stretching out on the bed beside Nathan and falling asleep.

That had brought the Manifesto meeting to an end, as far as Nathan could remember. He decided to visit his parents. He went back to his room to load his dirty washing into the bag he kept for the purpose. It had been one of those red and blue checked giant shoppers until Nathan painted it black.

The Pursey home, Genista, where Nathan had grown up with his two sisters, was a detached thirties house conspicuous for its window boxes, tubs and hanging baskets and the statuary in the front garden. Virginia creeper, clematis and passion flower raced each other up the façade and cradled the windows. Stone wheelbarrows full of pansies flanked the cartwheel gate set in a low wall, stone children offered baskets of flowers, and fauns and cupids peeped shyly through the foliage, the beds blazed with color, ivy, honeysuckle and roses tumbled over the pergola, sundial and birdbath and waterlilies floated on the pond among the koi carp fished by respectable gnomes. The rude gnomes donated by Nathan had been consigned to a shrubbery in the back garden where they mooned and exposed themselves to each other out of sight of the neighbors.

Nathan's father, Buster Pursey, designated himself The Floral King of the South-East. His own father had built the business from a barrow in Surrey Street market in Croydon and now Buster presided over the biggest flower stall for miles around, while the boarded-up shops of several local florists attested to his success. The extended family leased their own stalls and kiosks from Buster but they had their fingers in many other pies, and jellied eels, and anything that could be transported on a lorry with a dodgy tailgate. It tickled Buster that he shared the name of the "great" train robber who ran a flower stall at Waterloo Station, until the poor sod topped himself. If you saw an old-style gangland funeral procession winding along a South London street, the full monty, undertaker in a frock coat and top hat with ribbons walking in front of a glass-sided hearse drawn by black horses with nodding plumes, the odds were that the magnificent tributes that decked the coffin and the train of limousines had been supplied by the Floral King. The Purseys were past masters at seeing members of the criminal fraternity out with the respect they deserved.

The lives of the Purseys and the Cranes had become entwined when John Crane's aunt Maud had married Ambrose Pursey, Buster's uncle. It was an ill-starred romance, disapproved of by both families. Maud was a delicate girl who painted china at the Coulsdon Pottery and Ambrose had a shellfish stall in Croydon market. The couple were lost off the Kent coast on a cockling trip. They had no children and the relationship of the Cranes and the Purseys might have withered after the funeral service, but instead the tragedy strengthened it. Lyris had babysat occasionally for Buster and Sonia and she and John had taken their children to museums in the holidays. At John's funeral the undertakers had placed the Purseys' floral tribute on the coffin in preference to Lyris's hand-tied garden flowers, assuming that it represented the chief mourners. Sonia herself had designed the petalled artist's palette with dabs of color and a bunch of paintbrushes.

Nathan found his cousin Hayley in the kitchen with her baby Jack, having a cup of tea with his mum.

"Surprise, surprise," he said, dropping his bag on the floor.

"Nathan!"

Sonia Pursey rushed to fling her arms round her son, kissing his neck, which was as high as she could reach. Nathan was not tall, having the rather short Pursey legs and arms, but Sonia was just under five feet. Four feet eleven and three quarters to be precise, as she delighted to boast, pulling herself up to her full height to make herself look smaller. Buster called her his Pocket Venus. If he was the Floral King, Sonia had royal connections in her own right, numbering deceased Pearly Kings and Queens among her relatives. Nathan swung her off her feet.

"Blimey, Mum, you've put on a bit, haven't you?"

"Don't be so cheeky! I still buy my clothes in the children's department I'll have you know! These leggings are from Tammy Girl."

"I suppose that's your dirty washing," Hayley said. "Auntie Sonia was just saying you hadn't been home for ages."

"Here, son. There was just enough left in the pot. And Jaffa cakes, your favorite. I must have known something."

"Hullo, Princess, got a smile for your uncle Nat?" said Nathan, prodding baby Jack. "Is she walking yet?"

"Nathan!" said his mother.

"She's a he. And of course he's not walking, he's five months old. Your second cousin Jack, *if* you're interested. And I'd prefer it if you didn't spit biscuit crumbs on him, if you don't mind."

"Well, how am I supposed to know? There are so many sprogs in this family these days I can't keep up with it. Seems every time I turn my back one of you girls is about to pod."

"Nathan!"

"You *were* invited to Jack's christening. Not that you bothered to turn up or even acknowledge the fact."

Nathan dragged a thin roll of dirty notes from his jeans, peeled off a twenty and dropped it on to the baby.

"There you go, soldier. Christening present. Don't blow it all on Pampers."

Sonia beamed. Jack grabbed at the note as Hayley picked it up between finger and thumb.

"I'll put it in his Building Society. If they'll accept it in that condition."

"His little face!" said Sonia. "He's a real Pursey, that one. Reminds me of you, Nathan, when you were a baby. I'll never forget the time—"

"Spare us the Raw Mince story for the thousandth time, Mum," Nathan interrupted, winking at Hayley. Mimicking his mother's voice, he went on, "There he was, sitting in the middle of the kitchen, blood all over his little face, bless him, beaming like a little cherub. I didn't have the heart to smack him . . ."

"Good thing it was before this CJD scare," said Hayley, "except they're saying now the incubation period might be—well, I'd better be going, Auntie Sonia. Thanks for the tea."

"Hey, Hayley, did you see that piece about me in the *Sunday Times* the other week, about me and my mates and the crazy antics we get up to? Where is it, Mum? Give Hayley a copy to take home, it's a right laugh."

"She already showed me. I'm glad you think it was amusing. I'd be ashamed."

When Hayley and Jack had gone Nathan said, "Motherhood hasn't done much for her, has it? Sad. All my mates used to fancy her. She had it, she lost it."

"She's only jealous," said Sonia. "Morbid cow. Be a love and pick us a bit of rosemary. I'm doing a nice leg of lamb for later."

Nathan returned with a bunch of lavender.

"Thanks, that's beautiful."

"How are the girls, then? Been round lately, have they?" He was referring to his older sisters Lisa and Rachel, both married with children.

"Oh, yes," Sonia answered vaguely.

Nathan went up to his old bedroom and Sonia went into the back garden for some rosemary. She was so happy to have Nathan home that she almost used the lavender, and there was no way she would have drawn attention to his mistake, bless him.

Nathan lay on the faded Jungle Book duvet that Sonia kept on his bed and watched his paper lampshade, a pale blue globe with a map of the world, swaying in the breeze from the open window. The sun-baked cotton evoked memories of adolescent afternoons and he felt the tremor and throbbing that heralded all his best ideas. On this bed he'd wanked over his first Page Three Girl, smoked his first spliff, passed out after raiding the cocktail cabinet, cried when Mandy Rowlands dumped him. Nathan looked back with a fond sad smile at the little lad he used to be.

His idea was to construct a scale model of his bedroom, complete with a miniature teddy bear and plastic toys, a tiny spliff and a copy of the *Sun* open at page 3. There would be video games and Airfix battleships and planes, the smallest pair of trainers known to man. Better still, it could be a series of rooms, each depicting a stage of his life. His jeans were too tight to contain him. He undid the top two buttons. Art and sex were indissoluble. He tried to remember the name of the artist who was said to have painted with his dick. The lightshade was making half-turns on its flex, swinging to the left and back to the right. Nathan tried to concentrate on making a model of it from tissue paper and wire, and gave up.

Sonia couldn't resist running her hand over Nathan's orange hair. It felt soft, as it did when he was a baby with a yellow fuzz on his head like a downy little duckling. Nathan was sprawled face downwards on his bed. Sonia hated to wake him but dinner was ready. She patted his bottom. Nathan wriggled and sighed. Sonia shook his shoulder gently.

"Come on, sleepyhead. Dinner's ready and your dad's waiting."

Nathan lifted his head. There was a wet patch of dribble on the pillow and his eyes were bloodshot under their pink lids.

"Oh. Mum. It's you—I must've been dreaming." He yawned. "God, I'm really knackered. What's the time?"

"Dinner-time and I'm going to eat you all up!" Sonia replied, snapping her jaws as she used to when they played "What's The Time, Mr. Wolf?" "Come on, Lazybones, I'll race you downstairs!"

"You carry on, Mum. I just want to freshen up."

He couldn't move until she had gone because his flies were still undone.

"Two minutes, then."

This was how Sonia liked it, herself perched on her special cushion on her dining chair, carving the meat and passing heaped platefuls to her men. Except that Nathan was picking moodily at his food.

"Lost your appetite, son?" asked Buster. "State of him!" he said affectionately.

"Oh, he's been burning the candle at both ends, I expect," said Sonia. "Is that right, Nathan?"

"Dipping his wick more likely, eh son?"

"Buster! Do you mind? There are ladies present."

Nathan pulled the bottle of wine from the ice bucket and refilled his glass. He had glimpsed the girls' old dolls' house through a bedroom door and his plans had come crashing down. Doing his installation would just be like making a bleeding dolls' house. He remembered that Boxing Day when Mum and Dad had to rush him to Casualty when he'd got all his fingers stuck together with Superglue. Dad was done for drunk driving.

"Penny for 'em," said Buster.

Nathan regarded his father's straining T-shirt. The old man

must take a bigger cup-size than Mum these days. The way things were going, at the next family gathering they'd have to get a special table with semi-circles cut out to incorporate all the blokes' bellies. Maybe he should take the dolls' house after all; some of the furniture was bound to come in useful, particularly the bathroom suite, and he could do something ironic with the dolls. Then a vision of smashed glass blazed in his mind, of the house coated in a mosaic of broken mirror flashing points of light. Yes! That would show that old *shlemiel* Jacob Feinstein for dissing him last night, when you'd have thought he'd be grateful that somebody of Nathan's generation had even heard of *Kristallnacht*. People like that thought they'd taken out the concession on the war. Well, soon they'd have to reevaluate it from a nineties perspective.

"Eat up, Nathan. It's going cold. What's up with you, wriggling about on your chair as if you'd got ants in your pants?"

"You know the girls' old dolls' house?"

"Yes, funny you should mention it, Rachel's taking it for little Amy on Saturday. Kevin's going to do it up, give it a facelift."

"Tell them they can't have it. It ought to be a third mine."

The doorbell chimed.

"Now who could that be?" exclaimed Sonia, although unexpected visitors often called round at odd times to see Buster, sometimes getting him out of bed. He retired early as he had to be up for the market in the morning. Buster went to answer it, came back and jerked his head towards the front door saying,

"Guess who's turned up like the proverbial? It's for you, son. Tell her we're in the middle of our meal."

Before Nathan could leave the table Jackee Wigram was in the dining room.

CHAPTER FOUR

Clovis went out to buy a newspaper. Last night he had poured himself a stiff drink and watched *Newsroom Southeast* and later *London Tonight*. There was no report of anybody having been killed on an escalator at Green Park. It made a change from somebody throwing themselves under a train, but he supposed that if the person had merely been injured the accident would hardly be as newsworthy as an arson attack on a shop in Norwood, a shooting in Coldharbour Lane or a kitten called Lucky who had travelled unscathed from Beckenham to Whetstone on the undercarriage of a removal van.

He had woken to the memory of that curled figure on the staircase kicking feebly. Why had he done nothing to help? Because he had supposed the person was drunk? Anything he might have had to deal with would have been better than knowing he had let whoever it was—was it male or female?—be carried out of sight. His impression was of someone young, and male, in a sort of dirty khaki jacket, but he couldn't be sure. A busker or a homeless boy perhaps. Somebody's child. What if it had been Miranda and some man had stood watching her being taken up that grinding stair to God knows what? He would kill him. He had switched on the radio while he ran a bath and lay there listening to a song about a yellowbelly whom everyone considered the coward of the county. Candy had left it turned to Country 1035 AM when she called round yesterday.

★   ★   ★

Clovis sat at one of the pavement tables outside the Criterion Café with an espresso and the newspaper.

"You're out early, darling. Mind if we join you?"

It was Candy, on her way back from the park, holding a lead to which were harnessed five Tibetan terriers who jumped up at him. She kissed Clovis and tied the dogs to the leg of one of the white wrought iron chairs and sat down. She was wearing a man's white shirt belted over leopard-print leggings tucked into her dog-walking ankle boots, black patent with side zips and a two-inch heel. Her dry fair hair was tied back in a leopard-print chiffon scarf.

"So, do you just want to be left in peace with your paper?" Candy said when her hot chocolate and *pain au chocolat* had been brought. The dogs had subsided into a mat on the pavement. She lit a cigarette. Her voice had a husky edge, like the rough touch of her hair that reminded him of a bunch of yellow statice.

"Of course not. Why?"

"You seem very preoccupied. Or have you just got the glooms?" She spooned the last blob of cream into her mouth.

"I suppose I have. Sorry."

"Anything you want to talk about?"

"No. The thing is, I . . ."

Candy was looking sympathetically at him, her head slightly on one side. Listening to men's troubles was her forte. The flush that her walk had brought to her cheekbones had faded. Although she rarely left home without the full slap, today she wore no makeup except mascara and she looked tired. As if sensing it, she took a lipstick from her bag.

"Going to be another scorcher, after the rain last night. I've got a friend coming this afternoon," she said, stretching her lips as she applied the gloss, "but I'm around this evening if you fancy a drink."

"I might. Thanks. I'll see."

"Come on then, boys. But don't be a stranger, darling. Remember, a problem shared . . ."

When they had gone a sparrow landed on her plate to peck the *pain au chocolat* crumbs. There was a smudge of lipstick on her glass and a fringe of froth. Clovis wondered how she could face chocolate so early and on such a warm day, and remembered her saying once, "When life is bitter a little sweetness in the mouth can work wonders. Haven't you noticed how old people on buses are always sucking sweets?" He hadn't. If he had taken Candy to the party he would have been saved. They would have gone for something to eat and taken a taxi or a later train. If Candy had been with him on the escalator she'd have been over the handrail in a flash, dragging the boy from disaster and cradling his drunken head.

Candy would forgive him; it was her *métier.* But what would be the use of that? It wasn't Candy he had injured and she couldn't turn back the clock. "The Coward of the County" was still playing in his head, as it had throughout their conversation. Clovis had forced himself to listen to the song as if it were the beginning of his penance, and of course it had turned out that the coward had not been a coward at all when it came to the church. He thought he knew who the friend Candy was expecting would be.

Rayner Carmody, former Conservative MP, had lost his seat in the May election. Candy had been his mistress for more than twenty years and still believed that she was the love of Rayner's life, but then she would. Why had fate decreed, Clovis wondered, that a beautiful young woman should end up alone, pouring out her affection on a succession of little dogs? Candy had been working as a croupier in a Mayfair club when she met Rayner and bought into the mistress ethic lock, stock and barrel; her record collection was the national archive of anthems to forbidden love and female fortitude. While the rest of the country delighted in observing the death throes of an administration heaving with corruption. Candy kept the lid of her own little can of worms tightly shut. She cuddled up with the dogs on the sofa, wearing Rayner's favorite scent and waiting for his furtive calls, channel surfing for some schmaltzy movie when the sleaze hit the fan on the News. Rayner Carmody, father of four, was a weevil feeding on bread buttered on both sides. Had he thought, when he placed that first puppy in Candy's arms, that she wouldn't notice it was not a baby? A pup trailing a pink ribbon was all it took to buy off Candy's guilt about his wife and family. Why couldn't he have picked on somebody else?

CHAPTER FIVE

At about ten o'clock on the same morning Lyris was in the front garden tying back a Michaelmas daisy that had flopped over the path. She had stumbled on it the night before. Her garden was the antithesis of the Purseys', tangled green broken by smudges of color and the white of roses. The house was semi-detached and had gardens to the front and back and at the side which the studio overlooked. Last night's shower had refreshed the garden and, although sunny, the day promised to be less enervatingly humid than it had been for the last week. Lyris was wearing a long cotton robe and her hair was still in a loose plait down her back. She looked up suddenly, aware of being watched. The girl whom Clovis had called Nefertiti was leaning on the green gate in the high fuchsia hedge.

"Lyris? I know it's a cheek coming round so early, only Nathan gave me your address."

Lyris stared at the girl, affronted by the use of her first name and at being trapped in her own garden before she'd done her hair. The girl was wearing a white shirt over black trousers, with gold chains graduating in length until they disappeared into her coppery cleavage. Wedge-shaped brushstrokes accentuated the outside corners of her long eyes and the sun played in a crooked halo on the crown of her blue-black hair.

"Nathan Pursey? The artist? Your nephew?"

"I am well aware of who Nathan Pursey is, but I don't think you and I have been introduced."

The girl was inside the gate. A large black bag swung from her shoulder.

"Sorry. I'm Zoe Rifaat. I saw you at the party last night. Look, Lyris, I wonder if you could spare me a few minutes of your valuable time, only I'm researching a documentary series for Channel 4 and I'd really appreciate talking to you. Could we go inside the house for a few minutes?"

Lyris led the way through to the kitchen without speaking, shuffling a bit in John's slippers, kind boats that eased her aching feet. How typically too late all this attention for John was coming. Oh, if he were to be waiting there, doing the crossword at the kitchen table. Zoe sat down in John's chair, looking greedily round the room. Lyris poured two cups of coffee. Zoe admired the old fluted aluminum coffee pot and the painted pottery cups and saucers without realising that Lyris was speechless with fury.

"Let me explain," said Zoe. "As I say, I'm a film maker. Here's my card so you can see that I'm not some con-artist who goes round preying on the—" she laughed. "This is lovely, Lyris. You've no idea the crap coffee I have to swallow in my job. Comes with the territory. Maybe you saw my film about women's kick-boxing in Coventry last year? Anyway, the point is, Lyris, I'm making a documentary about neglected women artists."

Lyris's hair turned to cobwebs. She sat down.

"Neglected women artists?"

"Yes. Your name cropped up, and when I saw you at the private view last night and then when I met Nathan, it just seemed like it was all *meant*. Would you have any of your paintings handy, Lyris, that I could take a look at? You'll have to pardon my ignorance if I say I hadn't heard of you before"

The girl and her proposal were terrifying. Lyris wanted her

out of her kitchen. Nathan and Nefertiti in cahoots. Zoe was undoubtedly the most beautiful young woman who had ever sat at this old table and how Lyris willed her to go back to *Aida* or the British Museum or the set of *Carry on Cleo* or wherever it was she'd sprung from. And yet nobody last night had even acknowledged that she was a painter at all. Zoe laughed and patted Lyris's hand.

"No need to look so petrified. Let me explain a bit more. The idea's a sympathetic reassessment of women artists from the fourteenth century onwards, questioning why they've been so underrated in terms of male artists and hopefully reclaiming their place in history. You know, like why did it take so long for everybody to realise that Gwen John was a miles better artist than her husband? Is that what you'd generally wear for your painting, Lyris?"

"It's my dressing gown."

"Oh. Well it really suits you. I'd just have to have a peep at your pictures to get an idea of how they'd come over."

She sneezed. "You haven't got any pets lurking around by any chance? Only I'm desperately allergic to cats."

"I wonder what they think of you. Look, Miss Rifaat, you'll have to excuse me for a few moments while I get dressed. I can't possibly have this conversation with you until I do—your leather trousers place me at such a disadvantage. I was up extremely late last night—not that I see any reason to explain my *déshabillé*. Perhaps you could make some fresh coffee. And some toast. The bread's there. There's the grill."

That should stop her snooping around.

"No worries, Lyris. You take your time. And please, it's Zoe."

When Lyris returned in a two-piece of a shirt over a skirt patterned in overlapping black and gray squares, with her hair in a chignon secured with combs Zoe narrowed her eyes professionally.

"I think the other worked better, in your painting slippers and with your hair down. You looked more—painterly. Is that the word?"

"Not as I understand it."

"You're going to think me the most awful klutz. I couldn't understand how the coffee pot works. Are you supposed to unscrew it or what? And the gas wouldn't light so I'm afraid there isn't any toast either. Sorry. I've only ever used a toaster. You'll have to take my word for it I'm more proficient at the business end of a camera!"

"I usually find a match helps with the gas. Never mind though, we'll forgo the toast. It occurred to me—if you were to look at my work and find it demonstrably inferior to my husband's, would that affect your proposition?"

"I'm sure that won't be a problem, Lyris. You've got to believe in yourself, you know."

Lyris busied herself making coffee.

"You wouldn't have a biscuit, would you? Only I had to leave home so early I only had time for a Twix. South of the river's another planet to me so I was up at dawn, which didn't go down too well with Dan, my partner. Brilliant. Don't worry about a plate, I'll just—oh, thanks."

Lyris sat down at the table and lit a cigarette. With a grin, Zoe scrabbled in her bag for a pack of Marlboro Lights.

"Don't tell anyone. I'm supposed to have given up. I can't tell you what a relief it is to see that you smoke. My granny used to smoke sixty a day and she's—well she's in a home actually but . . ."

A mobile phone rang in Zoe's bag and she had a brief conversation.

"Sorry about that," she said to Lyris. "Do you mind if we get on with having a look at some of your pictures now, Lyris? I've got a meeting scheduled for one. Is that your studio, the room with the easel we passed on our way in?"

Zoe led the way back through the hall hung so thickly with paintings that no wall was visible.

"I was thinking," she said over her shoulder. "It might be a good idea to have Nathan in the film. Make it a bit controversial by intercutting BritArt with your work to show how times have changed and maybe get him to give his perspective on your work. And the fact that you're both related could give it a nice quirky angle. You have a think about it—I must just use your loo.

"Oh, and Lyris, I'd really appreciate it if you could let me have your CV. Just a couple of hundred words or so with a few dates, like when you were born and whereabouts. Education, any major prizes or exhibitions or examples of how your career was affected by marriage, whether it was a deliberate choice not to have children, any particular women artists you came into contact with over the years who influenced you. If you can let me have it over the next few days."

After Zoe had gone Lyris sat in the studio, in the balding velvet chair draped with a shawl where so many people had sat watching John painting them. His walking stick was hooked over the arm. Canvases were stacked with their faces to the wall like disgraced children. Zoe, while confessing to not having been particularly art-minded at school, had loved them. She had pulled a camera from her bag and snapped them.

Zoe's voice tolled in Lyris's head like a bell dragging the last syllable of each stroke. The girl had swooped at her on the doorstep and aimed a kiss, a faint garlicky puff of last night's wine, at her cheek. All this and Nathan too. Almost every member of the Pursey clan was a better artist than Nathan. She thought of the floral palette on John's coffin, which at first she had considered so embarrassingly vulgar, and which had then seemed heartbreakingly right, the brushes tipped with color against the flagrantly blue sky.

"Zoe," she had said, "I think you should know—Augustus John was Gwen John's brother, not her husband."

"Whatever. It's the same principle."

Lyris gripped John's stick. The wood was worn smooth by his hand. How dared Zoe claim that she was not a predator? Now she knew how those foolish people you read about in the paper felt, the so-called frail elderly who went into the kitchen to make a cup of tea for the friendly gas inspector, and later discovered their savings gone. Violated. Their isolation exposed. The telephone was ringing, and she let it ring. She looked out of the window at the back garden and saw a neighbor's cat sitting on the path.

"Where were you when I needed you?" she asked.

In the spring she had scattered a packet of squash seeds and now the side wall was a curtain of rough leaves and tendrils like green coiled springs hung with wry-necked bottle-shaped gourds, some long like cucumbers, some round and fluted. They ranged through the yellows from sunflower to pale gold with a silver pinstripe, primrose and ochre and gamboge tipped with a circle of green stripes. Their foliage trailed over the grass and looped the canes of red and yellow tomatoes. Lyris stared through the window until the yellows dazzled her, unable to think what else to do.

CHAPTER SIX

Jackee Wigram had suspected for some years that a malign force controlled her destiny. When she had met Nathan Pursey she had been employed by Home Acres in Acre Lane, Brixton, a Housing Association notorious locally for its cupidity, inefficiency and the cavalier way it dealt with its clients. Jackee had resigned on a matter of principle; the flat she had been promised had been given to the Maintenance Manager's sister-in-law. Jackee decided to go public, to blow the whistle on a raft of corrupt practices but nobody had wanted to know. The press wouldn't touch it and the council had blanked her.

Her boyfriend had dumped her soon after. Gary's parents, who had been born in St. Lucia, had disapproved and she didn't know if it was down to family pressure or because she hadn't got the flat that Gary had broken off their relationship. Whatever, she was left in her basement room in Herne Hill with no job, a broken heart and a head of dusty dreadlocks. She had got talking to Nathan in the crowd when Nelson Mandela visited Brixton. She told him she was a half-caste.

Things were never the same with Nathan after her parents turned up unannounced with a shower curtain and some cushions from Ikea. She couldn't really blame them, except that Mum needn't have flung the windows open with quite such enthusiasm. Fortunately Jackee was up, as she'd been out to buy some milk. Actually, the parents had been relieved that Nathan, or as much as they could see of him cowering under the duvet, was at least white; Mum and Dad were secretly every bit as racist as Gary's family. And she supposed they were pleased that he was male, even if he was an art student. They had never liked Jules either, but she was history now. Jackee burned as she overheard them talking in the kitchen while Nathan got dressed.

"I suppose she's going to go all artistic on us now," Dad said.

"Our poor little chameleon. When will she find her true colors?"

It was her mother who had reminded Jackee that she had a degree in Cultural Studies and suggested that she apply for a job in the library. Then she shamed her by saying, "We've still got your old painting set up in the loft somewhere. I could look it out for you if you like." Nathan had choked on his tea, splattering Mum's blouse. Jackee tried to tell herself that the distance between Herne Hill and Tufnell Park was the main reason for their break-up, even though it was she who had done most of the traveling, but in her heart she knew he had dumped her because he was bored. Jackee was working in the library now, and everything was starting to go wrong again. The other day she had seen Gary coming out of B&Q with a black girl and a baby. Gary was carrying two cans of paint.

When Nathan's call had come, waking her from sleep, it was the answer to a prayer. He sounded so desperate, crying and incoherent. Then when she finally got through to him on the phone the next day, he'd dropped it to the floor. Convinced that Nathan was undergoing some terrible crisis, Jackee had gone to his house straight from work. A nice Indian boy, not the usual sort to live there, had said that he hadn't seen Nathan since the day he moved in, when he'd noticed that he didn't look well. In a panic by this time, she had run round to the studios. Seb, Howard and Larry, none of whom she had wished to see ever again, were there. Seb told her that Nathan had gone off to meet some Egyptian woman at lunchtime. Jackee collapsed in tears. Then Larry said he'd spotted Nathan at the tube station carrying a big black bag.

"Do you mean that black bag he uses for his washing?" Jackee sniffed.

"Might have been. I can't say I've ever taken that much interest in Nathan's dirty laundry," said Larry.

"He's a fast worker," said Howard. "Meets a girl one night, next day she's doing his washing."

"Thanks," said Jackee.

She ran out to the sound of their derisive laughter. She knew that, apart from herself, there was just one person who did take an interest in Nathan's laundry. She spent the journey to Purley in an agony of trepidation, imagining Nathan in various states of mental and physical collapse. She dreaded seeing the Purseys again but Nathan needed her and she would be there for him.

Nathan was open-mouthed, a piece of meat dangling from his fork, as he stared at Jackee. After bursting into the dining room she stood, her face flushed, breast heaving, wild locks disheveled, panting at him.

"You've got a bit of explaining to do, young lady," said Buster Pursey, who had sat down at the table again. "Barging in like that. You nearly knocked me over on my own doorstep."

"Whatever happened to manners?" Sonia asked.

"I'm here for you now, Nathan. Everything's going to be all right now, I promise. I couldn't believe it when you said how I was the only one you needed. I've always been here for you and I always will be. Whatever it is, you can tell me."

"Do you know what all this is about, son? If so, perhaps you could sort it out so we can enjoy our meal in peace."

"Search me, Dad."

"Are you in some kind of trouble, Nathan?" said Sonia. She

turned on Jackee. "If he is, it's family business and none of your concern, so you can sling your hook."

"Can we go somewhere private to talk?" Jackee said to Nathan.

"No you can't. And you can sit down again at the meal table, Nathan. You're not going anywhere. If there's anything to be sorted we'll sort it here, as a family."

"You don't change, do you Sonia?" said Jackee. "What's so sacred about a bit of meat and two veg? You and your precious meal table and your precious family. Family, family, family. That's all that counts with you, isn't it?"

"That's right." Sonia's lips were thin and hard.

"I think you'd better leave, Jackee," said Nathan.

"No. I won't. Not until we've talked. Last night you said, you swore to me that—"

Buster interrupted, stabbing his fork at her. "I don't know what your game is, but if you've gone and got yourself pregnant, don't come round here trying to pin it on my boy."

"That's just typical of your vulgar, filthy, pathetic, *fat*, perverted mind! Last night your precious son was *begging* me, pleading and sobbing for me to take him back. I only came here because I thought he needed help. I never wanted to set foot in your hideous house again as long as I lived, and I'd rather *die* than have you for any baby of mine's grandfather! Or let *her* get her claws within a million miles of it! Well, sorry to disappoint you but I'm not pregnant and if I was you'd be the last to know."

"That's it. Get out of my house. Get her out, Buster. Now!"

Buster pushed back his chair, rose, and grabbed Jackee's arm, twisting it up behind her back, then pushed her towards the door while she screamed and tried to bite him.

"I'll teach you to insult my wife, you little slag!"

He jerked her arm higher. Jackee kicked him. He lifted her off the ground and ran her through the hall. Sonia and Nathan heard the front door slam.

"Pass me your plate, I'll pop it in the microwave. And your dad's."

When Buster came back Nathan said, "That was a bit hard, Dad, giving her the bum's rush like that."

"No more than she deserved."

"I know. It's stupid, but I can't help feeling sorry for her. I don't know how I could ever have . . ." He shuddered. "Oh well, we all make mistakes. Only I suppose I might have been a bit out of order last night, ringing her up. I'll know better next time. The thing is, Dad, I haven't got the faintest recollection of what I did say to her—I'd had a few bevvies at a party, as you do, been on to a club or three—but I swear to God I never asked to get back together with her. I mean, "begging and pleading"—she should be so lucky. Come to think of it, I've only got her word that it was me who rang in the first place. Who's to say that *she* didn't phone *me*? All I do know is, whatever *was* said, that sad Muppet Jackee has completely distorted it in her crazy mind. I reckon she's sick, Dad. She needs help."

"Help?" said Sonia, coming back holding their plates in her oven gloves. "They ought to lock her up and throw away the key."

CHAPTER SEVEN

Criterion Books had not moved with the times but there were people who preferred its scale and style, the clutter of second-hand, antiquarian and new, to those of the big bookshop chains, even if the stock was necessarily limited. Bibliophiles and readers whose intention was to purchase a book and nothing more were happy here, and if you were an old customer or came in with an interesting enquiry there was the chance of joining the proprietor in a drink or a cup of coffee at a pavement table outside the Criterion Café. From time to time an author, one who could be relied on not to attract much of an audience, gave a reading in the shop. The children's section was so small that it could accommodate only books personally approved by Clovis, and the back room, the width of a set of library steps, was narrowed further by books protruding from the shelves that reached the ceiling. Cascades of volumes threatened to fall and sometimes did, and the categorization was eccentric, but Clovis could put his hand on anything in stock. To the side was a scullery and tiny bathroom and a door which opened on to a yard where there was a brick shed which had been a workshop and now housed bits and pieces of old frames, empty cartons and a shifting population of urban wildlife.

After Candy left him at the café Clovis opened the shop and when he had scooped up the post, mostly catalogues and junk, he made himself another cup of coffee and sat down to distract himself with the crossword in one of the newspapers he had bought. The old-fashioned bell on the door jangled and a woman in a vest and cycling shorts came in; Clovis's instinct told him she was a time-waster. It had been such a hot summer that old ladies had taken to the streets dressed like little boys, queuing for their pensions in baseball caps and shorts.

"I don't suppose you have such a thing as *The Nancy Spain Color Cookbook?*" Clovis went into the back room and returned brushing dust from his knees.

"There you are, one Nancy Spain, slightly foxed."

"It does look a bit chewed at the corners. Is this the only one you've got?"

"There was another but it just walked off the shelf—some years ago. Unfortunately a fox got in last week and took a fancy to Nancy's recipes. Probably got a taste for them from the recent biog."

"I suppose it will have to do then. I presume you'll be knocking something off for its condition?"

"Sold as seen. Company policy, I'm afraid."

"I'll leave it then."

"Good idea," said Clovis. "The party menus wouldn't have worked anyway—you can't get the Windmill Girls now."

The trouble with young dykes today, Clovis considered, was that they had no wit, no style, no *camp*; granted there was the odd honorable exception who could still sport a tuxedo with panache or shimmer in bias-cut satin, but for the most part they were as cloney as cell-cultures and what was the point of that? You might think the *Rue Jacob* had never existed. Take Barb and Sam who lived down the road, the couple who had come in once to ask for *The Passiflora Press Guide to Backpacking in Holland*; amiable enough girls but they reminded him of nothing so much as a pair of those pecking ostriches you used to perch on the rim of a glass of water. Candy had been to one of their barbecues and claimed to have had a good time.

★   ★   ★

He made himself ring Lyris from the shop in the afternoon. His guilt was compounded by the realization that if he hadn't run out on her at the party he would not know anything about the incident at Green Park. He could hardly bring himself to speak, so as soon as Lyris answered he pretended that a customer had just come in. He was relived that Lyris seemed in no mood for a post mortem, if that was not an unfortunate expression, either, and he opened an envelope that looked as if it contained an invitation.

"I must just tell you," Lyris said, "the most frightful girl forced her way in here this morning—"

A fair girl in a khaki jacket flashed into Clovis's mind as Lyris went on speaking. "But of course you saw her last night. That Nefertiti girl. It turns out she's called Zoe and she's some sort of television director. I think she's bullied me into agreeing to something I know I'm going to regret."

Clovis pulled out the card, wondering what fresh hell—it *was* an invitation. To Izzie's fiftieth birthday party.

"Have you signed anything? No? Well you're in the clear then. Look, I really must go. Let's talk later."

One of his regulars, dressed in his book-stealing coat, had come in and was snouting through the 1930s schoolgirl stories. Izzie had scrawled "Do bring somebody!" on the invitation. How thoughtful. How vulgar.

Lyris put the telephone down feeling rebuffed. She supposed it had been a mistake to invite Izzie, but she had felt that she should; and she had wanted to talk to Clovis about Izzie's own invitation to a party in her cottage near Sevenoaks. She remembered Izzie mentioning it last night, along with a sad tale of a widowed neighbor she had taken under her wing. Strange how Izzie could always make one feel somehow less bereaved than other people. How was one expected to get to Sevenoaks, let alone a vague hamlet in the hills, on a Sunday morning without a car? The house was filled with dissatisfaction. She was uneasy and restless. She had tried to paint but Zoe's visit had ruined that for the day. Worry that the Lees had felt snubbed at the party stopped her from ringing Anne as she knew she should. Although they couldn't have heard Louis's disparaging comment, Lyris was as unhappy as if they had. The Lees hardly ever went Up West; they had made a special effort for her sake and Anne had bought a new dress. A fresh anxiety began fretting away: what if Nathan were to tell Sonia and Buster about the party? Would they be offended that no family had been invited? She glanced up and saw through the window Anne Lee opening the front gate. Anne walked up the path carrying a bundle of late runner beans, saw Lyris and smiled, lifting her hand in a wave that snatched a weight from Lyris's heart.

The Lee family lived ten minutes' walk away in Tivoli Road, a long street that snaked towards East Dulwich, coiling behind the private estate of town houses that had been named Jockin's Mead. Their friendship with the Cranes dated back many years to the time when Tony plumbed in the Cranes' first washing machine. John and Lyris agreed that Tony and Anne Lee possessed a quality rarely encountered now, that of contentment, which made them pleasant company; as John was painting their portraits, first Tony's and then Anne's, he became aware of a quietness surrounding them and birdsong outside the window while they sat motionless but for the thoughts passing across their eyes like clouds until chair and sitter were becalmed at the center of a still pool. It had been the Lees rather than the Purseys, for all their flamboyant flowers, who had kept Lyris going when the only thing she could do was pace the house and garden day and night wringing her hands, or sit motionless, huddled in one of John's old jackets, for hours on end.

Anthony Lee came from old gypsy stock. His ancestors were horse dealers and casual laborers, snarers of rabbits and eaters of hedgehogs baked in clay like gray horse chestnuts, repairers of farming implements and pots and pans; the women told fortunes and sold pegs and baskets packed with mossy clumps of violets and primroses from door to door. The Lees were renowned hawkers of herbal remedies, lucky charms, spells and love potions; each generation produced at least one son with a gift for dowsing and for finding the rare and magical mandrake plant that shrieked when it was plucked from the underworld by the light of the full moon. Or so it was told; in truth the earthy mannikin, priapic with fertility, was more than likely to have been carved from a forked root of white bryony.

Tony's branch of the family had gone into brick generations ago but kept their fondness for lurchers. Some of their new neighbors had spat at them and called "Pike" after them in the street and refused to serve them in the shops. Anne's people had been charcoal burners when much of southern England had still been forest. Tony and Anne were born within a few days of each other in King's College Hospital and, knowing little about their antecedents beyond two or three generations, considered themselves fairly typical South Londoners. Anne had been at school with Sonia Pursey, Sonia Brockley as she was then, and remembered her chiefly for her spiteful tackles on the netball court and her way of getting out of trouble by being the smallest in the class.

Sparrows had been building their nests under the Lees' eaves for as long as anybody could remember, while for some months now, visible only to themselves and their friends, a pair of inverted commas had hovered above the slate roof of the house next door, to show that Nancy Carmody and Rod Dyer had set up home there ironically. Rod and Nancy much preferred their original slates and windows but they had to envy the Lees' terracotta tiles and double glazing when it rained heavily. Tony and his sons Little Tony and Russell had built their extension and done all their home improvements themselves, working as a team as they did in the washing machine installation, renovation and repair business. They had plumbed in Nancy and Rod's Bosch in a neighborly way, even though Rod was not a Rod as they knew them, being something in computers, an anorak, as Russell called him, living over the brush with the daughter of a former Tory MP. In fact, his name was Roderick, not Rodney as they supposed. The young couple behaved like a couple of kids with a new doll's house. Anne and Tony had brought up four children, two girls and two boys, in their own home when it had been no bigger than the place that Rod and Nancy seemed to regard as some kind of joke.

Anne's whites, on the line before Rod and Nancy were awake, made theirs look gray, or pink or blue. It was not long before Rod complained about Tony's van blocking what he considered his parking space even though his car was in for repair. Apparently some friends visiting them had had to park in the next street.

"You'd have thought they would have gone for one of those houses in Jockin's Mead or Biggs' Coppice with an integral garage," said Anne.

She had seen Nancy in the front garden that morning.

"You're late today," said Anne.

Nancy worked in the publicity department of a publishing company. She was wearing a little gray single-breasted suit buttoned up to show a hint of black silky camisole, with a black rose pinned to the lapel, and her long auburn hair was piled into a velvet hat.

"I'm going to a funeral actually."

"Oh I am sorry. Was it anybody—close?"

"No. One of our authors actually. Suicide, sadly. Where's that bloody minicab? I'm going to miss the whole thing if it doesn't hurry up. I never met him but apparently he was the last person you'd expect to—do that. Always very smiley."

"One of those 'not waving but drowning' types, I suppose?"

"What? No, he used a Swiss Army knife. Apparently it was quite a mess. At last! Look at that, parked halfway down the road! Do you think this rose is a bit OTT?"

The minicab driver honked again and Nancy ran, calling back.

"By the way, we're having a washer-drier delivered next week. Could you have a word with Tony to see if he's interested in the old Bosch?"

When Lyris opened the door to Anne, she said, "Oh Anne, I'm so pleased to see you."

"I thought you might like some runners. They're the last. The rest of them have gone too woody."

"Do come in. I'll put the kettle on. I'd like your advice about something."

They went through to the kitchen. When Lyris had told her about Zoe's visit Anne said, "It's quite simple really. You say she claims to be allergic to cats, so get a cat. A long-haired Persian preferably. Or even two. I know of somebody who runs an animal rescue center and they're always looking for good homes. Some of the cats are quite feral."

An invitation to somebody's fiftieth was propped against a vase of poppy heads on the mantelpiece next to the green glass fishing floats. A trickle of brickdust pattered into the empty grate. Lyris's utensils stood in the old wooden rack on the draining board. Since John had gone Lyris had become ever more frugal, using and washing up the same saucepan, plate, cup and saucer, the one set of irons, like somebody really poor.

"John had a bad experience once with some television people, didn't he?" said Anne. "When they kept him hanging around all day in the snow at Crystal Palace and he caught pneumonia? They were making a program about some other artist . . ."

Lyris was looking as if she'd seen a ghost.

"But how dreadful of me. I'd quite forgotten that. How awful. Yes, of course he did. The Pissarro fiasco. It nearly killed him. You know he had TB as a boy? And then the film was never shown. How monstrously egotistical not to have remembered that."

"You mustn't blame yourself. We all forget things, I know I do. Sometimes it terrifies me, the things I don't remember about the children growing up, when at the time you think you'll always remember every moment. I feel that if *I* don't hold on to the memories they'll be lost forever. I really wish we'd had a video when they were babies. But then, Tony thinks we never really forget things; they're locked in there somewhere and we just have to know how to tap into them."

She tapped her forehead.

"How are those neighbors of yours?" asked Lyris. "The Anorak and Miss Nancy?"

"Oh, Rod's taken it into his head to have the apple tree in the back garden cut down. I don't know why he's bothered because they won't be there five minutes. He says it's a waste of space although I told him that those late frosts killed the blossom and it usually has a lovely crop of apples."

"You'll have to nip that in the bud."

"I'm doing my best. Tony reckons they've only moved here so that they can get their kids, when they have any, into one of the prep schools. I said, that's all very well but the kiddies from our school have to walk through the pollution caused by those au pairs and nannies driving their children to school, and it's not doing them any good. I met Nancy this morning, on her way to a funeral. She's a cold girl. Apparently one of their authors killed himself, poor chap, and she was more concerned about how she looked than about him."

"All those people with their fat salaries have no conception of life at the other end of their industries. They take more holidays than hairdressers. They should remember who pays for their fancy clothes. They pick people up when it suits them, make them jump through hoops and then toss them aside . . ."

"Like worn-out gloves," said Anne.

"Exactly. They should all be forced to reverse roles for a year or two and find out what it's like to grind out work for a pittance in the face of their demands and silences and sheer incompetence and ill-manners."

"The boot would be on the other foot then."

Anne did not know it but there was a carton of books in the cupboard under the stairs consigned in disappointment and anger to the spiders. The volumes representing John's work had missing indices and mistakes in the biographical details while in Lyris's case several color plates had been printed upside down. Anne was alarmed at the fury her story had provoked. Lyris's neck was corded with rage, her hands twisting the tea towel into a garrotte. Anne wondered who she was strangling. She could have bitten off her tongue for bringing up the Pissarro film. It wasn't like Lyris and herself to sit here pulling people to pieces and it didn't feel right. Suppose Lyris were to start exhibiting the early stages of Alzheimer's, how would she know what to do for the best? There was nobody else to call on, and it was only a year since she had buried her own mother. John had not been quite the full shilling when he died, although they had all glossed over it. One sandwich short of a picnic. Two colors short of a paintbox? It was hard to tell when someone had always been a bit eccentric. Remembering how they had wept together at this same table, she put her hand on Lyris's, searching for something comforting to say.

"It can't be easy, being creative."

"Oh well, it has its compensations, I suppose. If it were possible just to get on with it without engaging with the enemy. I suppose you don't know the poor fellow's name? No? Oh, well, unless he was somebody famous . . ." She smoothed out the tea towel. "A friend of mine, a painter, threw herself off Beachy Head, but it didn't make much of a splash . . . You'll be going back to school soon, won't you? It must be nearly the end of the holiday."

"Not for another couple of weeks yet. If I've still got a job with all these cutbacks. Anyway, I suppose I ought to be getting home."

She lingered, unwillingly reminded of their last dog Bonnie, a gentle rough-coated lurcher, in her basket with the tartan rug, and how towards the end they had hoped that she would simply not wake up one morning. But nature is seldom so kind.

"I'm going to Sainsbury's tomorrow. Is there anything you want to stock up on?"

"No, I'm absolutely fine, thank you. Of course, when I have my feral cats I'll probably be asking you to get me catfood in bulk and scratching pads to keep their claws sharp."

At the front door Anne said, "I've been meaning to say, it was a lovely party last night, Lyris. We really enjoyed it. Thanks very much for inviting us. I'm sorry we didn't get the chance to say goodbye, only you were surrounded."

"Oh no, thank *you* for coming. I so wanted you to be there and I know John would have too. Was the drive back all right?"

"Oh it was fine. We stopped off and got some chips. We hadn't done that for ages. Did you have a nice meal afterwards?"

"Let's just say that I wish I had had chips with you in the van."

When Anne had gone Lyris bit the top off a runner bean. The thought of preparing them, all those green curlicues in the colander, filled her with weariness. A bean fell on to the table, pink, spotted with black. She slit open the pod and removed three more beans. Scarlet, purple, mauve, speckled, perfect and packed with life, each with a tiny pale comma attached. What did they remind her of? Pebbles? Birds' eggs? A necklace of beads she had long ago? Every runner bean she had ever seen?

CHAPTER EIGHT

Nathan woke in his old bed and found a mug of cold tea on his bedside table. It was ten past eleven. He sensed that he was alone in the house and remembered his mother asking if he wanted to go with her to visit his Uncle Roy in Belmarsh prison.

"You evidently consider yourself a loveable old rogue, Mr. Pursey, although I doubt if your victims would agree with you," the magistrate had said, "but I must point out that the average age of the house-breakers we see in these courts is fifteen. Don't you think that perhaps it's time that you grew up?"

Nathan thought that yellow-toothed Uncle Roy must enjoy being banged-up, or why would he carry on when he was so obviously too fat for the job? He wondered what it would be like to be an artist-in-residence in a prison; what sort of art would murderers and sex fiends produce? Maybe it would just be like graffiti and tattoos. Or would they come up with images beyond anyone's worst nightmares? Could great art emerge from an evil psyche or would those guys' paintings be as bungled as their crimes? After all, they'd all got caught so they couldn't be exactly geniuses.

He and his mates used to laugh at video nasties while they were still at school; schlock-horror, virtual violence, cartoon rape, celluloid mutilation, but you could see a snuff movie on the Internet if you knew how to access it. What would it feel like to witness some vagrant or a street kid that nobody would miss actually die on your screen? He wasn't sure he had the stomach for it. He wasn't bottling out but he didn't fancy watching somebody dying to grease the pockets of a bunch of bastards in business suits and satisfy the lonely lust of sad drooling wankers. Those fuckers ought to fry. He'd pay to watch them sizzle, like you could in America. He'd throw the switch himself. He kicked off the duvet and went to have a bath.

Maybe the Net, that was the direction in which his art should be going, instead of dicking about with installations. It was time he had a personal website. All over the planet people he would never meet would be sitting at their terminals logging on to his work. It would be like having cybersex. He wished he could remember exactly what had happened with that girl the other night, and what her name was. Going global could solve all sorts of problems for him: that *Illustrated Dream Diary of a Young Artist* he'd been thinking about for example; if it was on CD Rom there would be no hassles with publishers or distribution, or even writing down the words. Nathan rubbed shampoo into his scalp and as he submerged his head it came to him. Zoe. Pieces of the evening began to float back and he remembered writing down Lyris's address in Zoe's snakeskin Filofax.

Sonia returned looking despondent.

"What's up, Mum?"

"I had a wasted journey. Visiting was cancelled. They wouldn't say why but I heard on the grapevine that another one had topped himself. One of those noncey-boys, I expect, but I suppose some mother will be getting a phone call."

"Mum, that's nonce, or Nancy-boy. Still, perhaps he's better off out of it either way."

"You're probably right. I say it'll be a good thing when they can identify people like that before birth, pick up on them on the antenatal scan. Save a lot of trouble all round. All this pedophilia that's about nowadays—you'd think those boffins would put their research into something useful—I mean, what's the point of wasting taxpayers' money on cloning sheep when there's no shortage of meat that I can see? They can't even find a cure for the common cold. Have you had anything to eat?"

"You know me, Mum. What time's Dad home? I've got to ask him about something and I don't want to leave it too late to get back."

"Oh, Nathan, you can't go yet! You've hardly been here. And your dad's booked a table at La Perla for tonight. It's all arranged—the girls are coming, it's going to be a real family do. You can't disappoint everybody."

"Just tonight then. I've really got to get back to work."

"Thanks sweetheart. I don't suppose you feel like running the mower over the lawn for me, do you?"

"I don't mind."

"Promise you won't do anything anarchistical this time, like cutting it into a checkerboard? Remember it's only a lawn, not a symbol of bourgeois decadence."

Sonia watched from her lounger as Nathan, his chest anointed with the factor 10 sunscreen she'd smoothed into him, followed the Flymo up and down the green stripes. He looked lovely and clean. She'd slipped a pair of Odor Eaters into his trainers while he slept.

"By the way, that Jackee had the gall to ring whilst you were still in bed. She got a flea in her ear from me."

"Thanks, Mum, you're a star."

CHAPTER NINE

The cotoneaster, gemmate with red berries, had spread in a peacock's tail over the grass. Lyris habitually read into the small hours and the cotoneaster brought back a sentence from the book she had fallen asleep over the night before: when Edith Sitwell was a little girl she had walked arm-in-arm with a peacock. Then she became a peacock herself. Lyris was sitting in the sun outside the open studio door and the thought of the metamorphosis made her smile. She watched the grave, measured steps of the lonely child and the bird with its viridescent tiara progressing down a wide path through the topiaried gardens; to have made herself into a bejeweled poet was the best revenge that odd child who was told she was ugly could have taken on the unhappy years. Was that what the peacock had advised her to do? Surely he was wiser, that feathered tutor who took her under his wing, than the arrogant father who had devised a contraption to bend soft young bones into a shape that would be acceptable to him, like a gardener shackling an espaliered sapling. And how dared that impertinent Zoe Rifaat ambush her with questions about her own childless state? And how could it have slipped from her mind like snow that John had almost died of pneumonia while making that film?

She had longed for a baby and she had never conceived. John had longed for a child too. They had assumed they would have children, and they hadn't had. The lack, or the loss as she felt it, the ache, had bound them closer together and if either ever wondered if a different partner might have provided the child that was so deeply desired, the thought remained unspoken. Besides, they had been blessed, and not always so blessed, with the company of friends' children and grandchildren.

During the war, with no duty of care towards any children of their own, Lyris and John had been accepted as official War Artists, and were transported with the troops to Normandy. John had served too alongside the crew of a submarine, the history of tuberculosis which had kept him out of the Armed Forces proving no hindrance to that. Previously Lyris had a job with the Ministry of Food working on the Committee for Vegetarian Interests which ensured that non-carnivores were provided with appropriate rations. A couple of years after the war they joined a community of artists in a large house in Walberswick on the Suffolk coast. It was a period of shared recupera-tion and hope, of the reclamation of the English shore for Peace as they discovered the jagged, spiky plants, the tough little flowers that had broken the shingle regardless and sprawled over the skeletons of lobster pots and rolls of rusting barbed wire. The women made shiny transparent underwear from surplus parachute silk and dresses from bolts of blackout material. John and Lyris swam and dug fortifications with the children of the community and decorated sandcastles with chips of cornelian, shells and feathers and walked for miles inland, through reeds, and along the beach, wearing thick sailors' jerseys against the wind, in the light pouring from racing skies, to Snape and Aldeburgh where music was being made. Driftwood flared with mineral flames; samphire, glassy green and salty, tasted of the sea, jugs of ale bubbled on the kitchen table.

A branch of driftwood and a lobster ended the idyll. There had been rifts already; Lyris had noticed that it usually fell to the women to shop, wash the heavy fishermen's smocks and jerseys and clear the ash from the grates and rinse the grit from samphire and kale. Unless they were all to go hungry in squalor, the women, and chiefly herself, had to be housewives before they could begin to paint, carve or weave. The driftwood was a long branch polished and sculpted by the sea into the shape of a horned sea serpent. John and a painter called Alastair quarreled like schoolboys over who had seen it first. "Finders keepers, losers weepers," Alastair repeated, jabbing the stem of his pipe at John's chest; he was assembling a pyramid of *objets trouvés* on the shoreline.

Later that evening Lyris snatched a live lobster from the hand that was about to plunge it into a pot of boiling water. She ran down to the beach holding it at arm's length while it flailed and clamped its claws on the air. Alastair's wife Colette accused Lyris, over the head of the baby she was feeding, of being too immature and selfish to adapt to life in a community.

"You'd do anything to draw attention to yourself, wouldn't you, even if it means the rest of us starve. Don't think I haven't seen you dancing in the wind, giving yourself Yeatsian airs."

"Selfish?" said Lyris. "At least I don't boil dirty napkins in the soup pan."

"Huh! I pity you, Lyris. It's so pathetically obvious that inside you're embittered and eaten up with envy because you are barren. It wouldn't take a psychologist to deduce that from your warped, immature little paintings. Have you considered that you're being grossly unfair to John in tying him to you? And anyway, you'll never be a true artist because you'll only ever be half a woman, a withered old harridan venting her spite on the young and fertile."

Lyris shrivelled. She was a strand of dried seaweed, a brittle whelk-egg case blown along the shore. She had no recollection of dancing in the wind. At first light she and John started on the journey back to London. Lyris had confided in Colette her disappointment that she had not become pregnant yet; she had thought of her as a friend. And all the time Colette had hated her. As she wept on the train

John tried to make her laugh, saying that Colette, who had tow-headed, neglected twins as well as the new baby, was just a greedy old crab disappointed with her prey, who had lashed out with her own pincers. "I'll tell you what," he said. "Our children will be a damned sight better looked after than those poor kids of Colette and Alastair's. And better-looking too. We'll have ten, just to spite them. She's just jealous because she knows you're a far better painter. And more beautiful." As the years passed Colette's words sometimes came back to haunt Lyris like a curse.

Even if she had not rescued that lobster, Lyris would not have joined in the cracking and sucking of its boiled carapace. She was the child of two fruitarians who lived until they were a hundred years old. What acres of grain, what orchards, what fields of sunflowers they must have consumed before they became part of the landscape for ever. Mother and Father, fruit farmers and Fabians; gray good-natured horses put out to pasture. As she sat in the sunshine Lyris lit a cigarette and reflected on their longevity and sighed: what on earth was she to do with the years that stretched ahead?

She was thinking about the Eskimos who set their old people upon an ice floe and pushed it out on a voyage of no return into the freezing arctic sunset. She supposed the old ones were complicit in the ceremony, having always accepted it as an inevitable rite of passage, but how did they know when the time had come?

What if a person wasn't ready to go and screamed and struggled, shouting hoarse pleas to blank-faced grandchildren as the gap widened between the shore and the black ice-flecked sea, feet sliding on the floating bier, bleeding fingers slipping, losing their grip?

Anyway, she had no family nearby to set her adrift, and ice floes were rare on Dulwich Park pond. Her only brother Fabian (meaning Bean Grower) was in New Zealand; he had a grandson who was studying marine biology. Young Adam would be the boy to consult when she was ready to go; he would know about tides and coastal movements and where to find a warm but treacherous sea where one could avoid officious dolphins who might insist on snouting one back to the shore. The beads of the cotoneaster returned her mind to the painting she was working on; there a single roughcast bead must burn blue in a desert landscape.

CHAPTER TEN

Jackee was sitting at the information desk in the library picking her nails and staring blankly at the letter in front of her. She had got in late, still punch-drunk from the previous evening, outraged and humiliated almost beyond bearing, with Sonia's mouthful of abuse down the phone echoing in her ear. A tableau of the Purseys at their meal was fixed in front of her, like a slide stuck in a projector, Nathan with his fork poised, his open mouth full of meat. She could still feel Buster's arm across her breasts, a great male sinewy hairy thing scrunching them as if her body was garbage, a black sack of rubbish hurled towards the dustbin. She had felt something break inside her, not just the round mirror in her pocket but an invisible part of herself.

"You look like something the cat's dragged in. Go and do something to yourself before the public sees you in that state," Marsha the library manager told her.

Jackee mumbled something about a hangover, hoping it would suggest she had a life.

"You ought to get out more, girl. Drinking on your own's no good for you, you know."

Jackee felt like a cockroach crawling across the floor to cry in the washroom. Sometimes she thought Marsha picked on her just because she was white, but of course that couldn't be the case. She feared, admired and envied Marsha Campbell-Bellingham. As she wiped her nail-bitten fingers on the paper towel, Marsha's nails, long, curved and pale blue with a sparkle of rhinestone, flashed before her, reminders of the unbridgeable gulf between them. Jackee had tried; when she started the job she had bought some Hard Candy nail varnish but at the end of each day she had chewed so much off that she must have eaten nearly a whole bottle.

"You're not supposed to take it literally, you know," Marsha had told her.

Jackee read the letter again. It was from the head of the local school. Much of Jackee's job consisted of sorting out muddles caused by her own and others' maladministration, but she was also responsible for promoting Literature and Reading Skills in the community. She was in the process of organizing a Festival of local writing, but so far all the authors she had approached had blanked her.

> Dear Ms. Wigram
>
> I am writing to request you not to send any more storytellers or entertainers to Lydia Teesdale Infants. A designated Failing School facing the threat of closure which has been pilloried in the national media, our last OFSTED inspection was marked by a series of disruptions leading to classroom chaos. Additionally, dyspraxia is one ongoing problem which we are trying to tackle at Lydia Teesdale and negative role models such as The Dropped Balls Juggling Troupe seriously undermine our Confidence-Skills-Building Project . . .

Jackee skimmed the rest of the letter in despairing disbelief. She had sent the storyteller in good faith, believing Anancy the Spider to be a key member of the cultural diversity team, and now she was held responsible for a child being statemented for arachnaphobia. And she stood accused of causing an outbreak of face-paint dermatitis.

A pair of hands smelling of coal tar soap covered Jackee's eyes. "Surprise, surprise!"

"Dad!"

"Hello, Princess. I was making a delivery in the area so I thought I'd bum a cup of coffee off my favorite daughter. I'm in the smoke alarm game," he explained to Marsha, who was staring at him.

"Can you cover for me for fifteen minutes, Marsha? Please!"

Jackee turned a desperate look on Marsha, while surreptitiously tapping her forehead to imply that she was following some library procedure for dealing with loonies with delusions of paternity.

Dad caught her at it and she had to scratch her head vigorously.

"About time you did something about your hair, Princess. It's starting to look like something you sweep out from under the bed." He winked at Marsha.

"Will that be OK then, Marsha?" asked Jackee.

"'Course it will. You can cope without the boss for a few minutes, can't you, sweetheart?" said Dad, winking at Marsha again.

"Be my guest," said Marsha.

As Jackee led her father out he said, "Authority, Princess. Number one rule in management/staff relations. Don't ask 'em, tell 'em. Otherwise how can you expect your workforce to respect you?"

Seated at a table in Millie's Café, Jackee clenched her fingers on the letter from Lydia Teesdale School which she had thrust into her skirt pocket. While her father was at the counter getting the coffees and two Danish with apricots like poached eggs, she smoothed it out and reread it. The head's signature jumped off the page. Melody Eatwell. She had been at school with a Melody Eatwell.

When Jackee returned to the library she sidled behind the information desk and binned the letter. Marsha confronted her.

"You lied to me. You told me you were a half-caste. If your dad's from Barbados I'm Princess Diana, *Princess*."

Jackee opened her mouth to protest that he wasn't her father but an abusive lover of her mother's who forced her to call him Dad, but none of the excuses she'd cooked up in Millie's would come out. Tears prickled her eyes at Marsha's mocking use of her dad's pet name for her.

"You're pathetic, you know that? You're nothing but a white nigger. We laugh at wiggas like you, you know. I'm going to call you Jackee Wigga from now on. You know something? I feel sorry for your dad having a daughter who's such a liar, making out he's black. Are you ashamed of him or what? And passing yourself off as the library manager, that's a disciplinary offense in itself, right?" Jackee wiped her eyes on a sticky paper napkin but Marsha had only paused for breath. "You want to take a look at your Bible, man—Honor thy father and thy mother, yeah? How am I going to trust you in anything now? How do I know you didn't fake your references or whether any of the details on your application were the truth? I reckon you only call yourself Jackee because it rhymes with ackee."

Jackee put her hands over her ears. The children at her primary school had called her Jackie Wigwam. She could hear them now, circling her in a mocking Red Indian, no, Native American, dance, uttering war cries before they tied her to a tree. As she rocked in pain, she felt something spongy yet solid under her fingers of her right hand. A malignant growth? Marsha would have to be sorry now. The lump came away in her hand and she pulled it fearfully through her nest of hair.

"My lucky rubber! I wondered where it had got to."

"Thought you knew it was there. We've all been calling you Eraserhead for days."

Jackee noted the excluding "We" and a tear spilled as Marsha said, "Shows when you last washed your hair."

She would give in her notice, take a bit of time out to consider her options, maybe write a leaflet on "Scapegoating in the Workplace."

"I'm talking to you, girl. Don't just sit there giving me attitude!"

Jackee looked up.

"You realize that what you did is disrespectful to all black people, right? Black comes from the inside, you know."

"I'm sorry, Marsha. Really sorry. I never meant to diss you, honestly. I would never disrespect you. You've got to give me another chance so I can prove it to you."

"You had your chance, girl, and you blew it."

"I'll clear my desk then. Shall I?"

Marsha took a Cloret from the packet on the desk and crunched it.

"Hate to have to point it out, but it ain't your desk, Ms. Wigga. I'm going for my break now. You were out with your dad for twenty-seven minutes, so I'll be adding that on, which will give me time to consider your position. There may be Procedures to be followed and you've given me no option but to check out the terms of the Race Relations Act to see if you've committed a statutory offense. Also, you may not have noticed but there are three people waiting for attention. I'll see you later."

"La'er," mumbled Jackee. "I mean, see you later."

She couldn't look at the readers who had witnessed her disgrace and ducked her head to scrabble through a desk drawer. Lexie, one of the library assistants, came to her rescue.

"OK, who's first? How can I help you?" adding to Jackee, "You could make a start by booking a hair appointment to have those dreads cut off. Aside from they're really old-fashioned and they don't suit you, there's no point now is there, as Gary dumped you ages ago, didn't he? You could look quite reasonable if you did something about yourself. Improve your interpersonal skills, get some decent clothes or at least buy yourself an iron. Lose a bit of weight, sign on at a gym. I go line-dancing with my boyfriend three nights a week . . ."

"Excuse me for butting in, but I thought this was an information desk." Some old geezer in a Panama hat was flapping a bus map.

"So what was it you wanted? I'm officially on my break you know," Lexie said.

When Jackee forced herself to analyze the incident later in the comparative safety of her flat, it seemed to her that Marsha's expression had had more pity in it than anger, and she thought she had heard the faint sound of Marsha laughing like a drain in the washroom. Four Dime bar wrappers littered the sofa; four unopened bars were stacked on the arm. A full ashtray on the floor waited to be kicked. She had the remote in her hand so that she could change channels when a thought became too painful. At least if Marsha *had* been laughing at her she wouldn't have to face the Race Relations Board. To be called a racist was unbearable. How could Marsha be so wrong about her? It wasn't fair; why was it OK for black people to go blonde but if she wore a black style she was committing an offense? There was no way she could even go into a hairdresser's, she felt sick at the thought of facing all those skinny scornful people. She would have to cut her hair herself, if she could get off the sofa. Beyond her closed curtains there was an evening going on and she was trapped in an oblong of negative air like a pensioner afraid to venture out after dark. Her body lay inert, sickened with chocolate, but her mind was flinging itself round the room, beating its head against the walls, ripping down curtains and smashing glass with bleeding fists.

Jackee scrolled through the names of people she might turn to: Mum, Dad, Marsha, her old girlfriend Jules, Gary, Nathan, Nathan's sister . . . the impossible list. Lyris Crane's wise, kind face flickered and vanished. A rock of crack, cocaine, heroin, dope, Doves, E, alcohol—there was a medicine cabinet full of painkillers out there on the street, substances that made you thin. She would be less judgmental next time anyone came into the library out of their head. Maybe she should ask her doctor to put her on Prozac, but he was always off sick when you tried to get an appointment. If there was only someone, one person, a friend, a girl or some gay guy to be her best mate, a little baby even, to love her more than anybody else in the world forever. It was terrible to have passed through so many incarnations, schoolgirl, student, care worker, housing trust officer, dyke, library assistant and not to have retained a single friend from any of them.

The sudden certainty that her father's visit had not been as impulsive as he'd made out and that her parents guessed at her loneliness propelled her off the sofa in pain and shame, tripping on the ashtray, to find her scissors and attack her locks in front of the bathroom mirror. She remembered the smashed pocket mirror and the suppressed truth surfaced; that when Daddy had come into the library, beneath her horror was the impulse to fling her arms round him like a child who runs out of the playground in tears with a satchelful of broken treasures. It had been dreadful, sitting in the café trying to force down a Danish pastry while he called her his Princess, knowing the filthy names Sonia Pursey had shouted at her, bruised by Buster Pursey.

Some of the extensions had rotted and came away easily, others were glued agonizingly to her scalp. She hacked until all that was left was a frizzy cap for her own dyed hair. A pale face stared at her from the mirror, saying, "Well I hope you're all satisfied now." The basin was full of dusty twists and hanks.

"Who are you?" Jackee asked the face in the glass.

CHAPTER ELEVEN

It was not that he had absolved himself, but short of returning to the scene of the crime and making enquiries, there was nothing Clovis could do. As the day went on the figure on the escalator began to lose focus and the tube train doors that had sealed him in with his guilt seemed less symbolically dramatic. Had those hissing rubber lips been black or gray? While he admitted his culpability, he began to think that he had over-reacted and really the whole thing had been comparatively minor. Just another run-of-the-mill metropolitan fiasco with possibly no damage done. Perhaps good would even come of it if some kid learned the sharp lesson that it's a bad idea to go careering around on the underground out of control.

It was absurd even to think of Miranda in those circumstances, at the mercy of a Bad Samaritan, a Levite or whatever, because Miranda would never put herself in such a position. The only thing Miranda might have in common with that young person was fair hair, and Miranda's was cut in a shiny bob that brushed the shoulders of her school pullover. If he himself was soiled and tainted, nobody but he need ever know.

"Everyone considered him the Coward of the County"—if only that damn tune would stop playing in his head. Candy's taste in music was execrable. He would go round later though, he decided; he could use some company. He turned on the radio, filling the shop with Ligeti's "Sonata for Solo Viola."

"So are you going to Izzie's party then?" Candy called from the kitchenette where she was struggling to stop angel-hair pasta from escaping through the holes of the colander. She was making her stand-by *spaghetti alla puttanesca.* Minus the anchovies, because she'd given the last tin to the dogs.

"I suppose I'll have to. For Miranda's sake. I can't imagine why Isobel is putting herself through this. You'd think she'd have acquired enough wisdom in half a century to know that parties always end in tears."

"Some people enjoy giving parties."

Clovis came to lounge in the doorway, smoking a Black Russian Sobranie he'd taken from the silver box on the coffee table, watching Candy scraping a jar of pesto on to the pasta. He reached over and stole an olive from the chopping board. "Not Izzie. She'll be a nervous wreck for weeks before the event, exhausted and running around like a headless chicken on the day, then she'll lie awake all night worrying that those of her guests who don't die of food poisoning will be killed or done for drunk driving on the way home and she'll spend the rest of her life agonizing over somebody she forgot to invite or unwittingly snubbed."

Candy licked the pesto spoon before throwing it into the sink. They carried the bowls of pasta and salad through to the coffee table. Candy sat on the sofa with her plate on her knees while Clovis was in an armchair with his glass on a reproduction Jacobean table beside him. The room was lit by shells of peach-colored glass on the walls and a yellow lava lamp on another three-legged table; pairs of miniature dogs were dotted about; a night breeze stirred the curtains at the open window but at nine o'clock the air was warm and humid. The Eagles'

"Hotel California" coming softly through the stereo played its familiar surreal little film in their minds.

"Is she still working for that hedgehog charity?"

"I imagine so. She's just become a magistrate though."

"Blimey. You'll have to watch your step now."

"Oh I do. I do. This is excellent."

"So how many people has she invited?"

"I've no idea. Why are we spending the evening talking about Izzie? Do you want to hear about our first date? I took her to see *Whatever Happened to Baby Jane?* She was in such floods of tears we had to leave the cinema and she sobbed all the way home."

"Well it *was* quite sad. Those two wasted lives, and Bette Davis dancing on the beach like a demented birthday cake, and that song—" Candy began to croak brokenly, "I've written a letter to Daddy, his address is Heaven above . . ."

"Enough already. She was crying for the rat."

"The rat?"

"The rat that Bette Davis served up for Joan Crawford's lunch."

"I see. Clovis, I'm a bit worried about Sherpa. His back legs are going again."

Clovis had seen the dogs sleeping in a nest on Candy's bed when he'd hung up his jacket. Two wasted lives. As he'd missed the end of the film he couldn't comment, but it struck him that the description might apply to Candy and himself.

"Take him to the vet for another cortisone shot. He'll be fine. They're pretty tough, those Sherpas. Have to be, to keep climbing up and down Everest."

"I suppose. But he's not a young doggie any more."

"Like the rest of us. Nice flowers," said Clovis, nodding towards the vase on the bookcase.

"Yes, if you go for dyed blue chrysanthemums from a service

station. There was a time when he had a standing order for roses at Moyses Stevens. I've hardly seen him since he lost his seat."

"What about his directorships and consultancies, surely they bring him to town?"

"Occasionally, yes, but he seems to do a lot of it from home now."

"At least you don't have to worry any more about paparazzi shoving their lenses through the bedroom window."

It was extraordinary how the previous government had disappeared so completely. Now that they were in Opposition it was as if they had never been. No longer any fear of that "I'm standing by him" photo-call, wifie and kiddies leaning on the farmyard gate with hidden cattle-prods in their backsides to make them grin, or of Candy's face caught off-guard in cruel close-up lining a million litter trays. Clovis poured more wine, although he feared they were getting into maudlin time. Candy's eyelids were heavy and she was singing along under her breath, identifying with the girl in "Lying Eyes"; that lyric always got her—"I feel as if I've been living on the cheatin' side of town all my life," she had told him once. He knew that Candy was a few drinks ahead of him, but he was in danger of unburdening himself about the escalator. "I guess every form of refuge has its price," sang Candy, nodding sadly.

"Did I ever tell you about the time I went to Rayner's place in the country years ago?" she asked.

"Yes."

"It was the worst weekend of my life. I should never have gone but I was curious. And I admit it, jealous. I had to pretend to be with Tufty Cunninghame-Piggott, you know, who had to resign over that pork pie affair. The worst thing was, I asked Rayner what I should wear, and he said, "Oh we all just muck around in old jeans and jerseys with holes in the sleeves, sort of thing." So I thought, that's all right then, although I didn't have any jerseys with holes in them. What he didn't tell me was he meant *cashmere* jerseys."

"So there you were in borrowed wellies three sizes too big and both elbows sticking out of the holes you'd snipped in your acrylic tunic top . . ."

"Oh stop me if you've heard it before. Anyway it was all hideous. Have *you* ever tried to get pigshit out of white stretch jeans? And that horrible kid Nancy, I'm sure she twigged. I was prepared to believe it was an accident the *first* time she rode that pony over my foot and I do think Rayner might have warned me that one of their dogs was called Candy, an ancient golden labrador with a bandaged tail."

"I don't suppose you'd want to come to Isobel's party then?"

"What? Are you serious? I'd love to."

Another one bites the dust, thought Clovis.

"We'll have to get her a gift. Something really special."

"Giving a present is an act of aggression," said Clovis. "How dare anyone presume that one will rearrange one's pictures to accommodate some interloper, or make time to read some book, or wear some article not of one's choice or tend some discordant bloom? The only acceptable presents are ephemeral."

"Fifty red roses then. Or one of those facsimiles of a newspaper that came out on her actual birth date. Four cases of wine, with two extra bottles on top. A ginormous flask of her favorite scent, or a pipe of port."

"Fifty pence. A pipe of herb tea. A family-size bottle of *Eau de Hedgehog.*"

"Oh, you're impossible. Is this the Clovis I know and love, or his evil twin? You've better leave it to me."

CHAPTER TWELVE

"Nathan, do you have to hoover up your spaghetti like that? It's really putting me off," said Lisa.

"What? This is how you're supposed to do it, not with a knife and fork."

Nathan glanced at Lisa's husband Sean, who scowled.

"At least he's not splattering everybody else with tomato sauce."

The Purseys were seated at the long table in La Perla, Buster at one end, Sonia at the other, the grown-up children bickering among themselves.

"Leave it out you two," said Sonia. It was just like old times. Her eyes sparkled as she looked fondly at Nathan eating; she had always known he would be artistic from the way he had played with his food when he was a little boy. She was wearing a sleeveless V-neck top in a crunchy gold knit with a metallic sheen and a heavy gold necklace and bracelets that set off her tan. Buster and Nathan were in shorts and vests, Buster with a gold chain and Nathan with a candy necklace. It was a warm fleshy evening of Neapolitan love songs, moist skin and escalopes beaten into the shape of the map of Italy, the fountain trickling in the grotto by the bar. The party consisted of the girls and their husbands, Hayley and her husband Richard, one of Buster's brothers-in-law Leslie and his wife Pat and several Pursey *bambini* with noses as yet like button mushrooms, one infant trapped in a high chair and the others running around the restaurant crunching breadsticks into the carpet until they were called to the table.

A couple at an adjacent table asked for their bill and left without ordering a main course. Buster waved an empty bottle at the waitress.

"You're quiet in here tonight, Serafina," he said. She side-stepped the hand reaching out to pat her bottom.

"I'm not Serafina. Funny, we were really busy a little while ago."

"I don't know where your boss has been getting his table decorations but you'd think he could do better than a sprig of heather and bit of dead maidenhair. Tell him I want a word."

"Mum, have you seen Lyris lately?" Nathan had to raise his voice to make himself heard. "Only I—"

"Funny you should mention Lyris. I was thinking only this morning, there she is, rattling around in that empty house—she's not getting any younger, is she?" put in Buster. "I mean, I wouldn't like her to be taken advantage of."

"How do you mean, taken advantage of?"

"Think about it. Old dear all on her tod in a valuable piece of property, nobody much to leave it to. Maybe losing her marbles a bit as time goes by, no disrespect. Houseful of pictures we don't know the value of but if I remember rightly some of them are by quite famous artists so they're bound to be worth something, might even be some Old Masters tucked away among them, and friend Lee and his missus with their feet well and truly under the table. So where does that leave the family at the end of the day?"

"Surely it's up to her what she does with it?" said Hayley.

"Well, of course it is. I'm not saying that." Buster chewed as he spoke. "What I mean is, *if* she's compost mentis to decide. But she could be got at, *persuaded,* her arm twisted by somebody unscrupulous. Look at it this way, Hay, Lyris is a vulnerable old lady, her nearest relatives are in New Zealand and they can't look out for her, so I reckon it's down to us as next of kin. Personally, I wouldn't trust that pikey Tony Lee further than I could throw him."

"Well, I think it's wicked to prey off old folk who can't look out for themselves," said Sonia. "I never cared for Anne much at school. She was supposed to have gone to the grammar only her parents wouldn't stump up for the uniform. What would she know about art anyway? If anybody ought to get his hands on those pictures it should be Nathan."

"Nathan's not the only person in this family even though you might think so." Rachel, whose face had grown redder throughout the conversation, looked at her sister for support.

"Oh, isn't he? My mistake, I always thought he was," said Lisa.

"Shut it, you two. Nathan's in the art game, that's the point. Those pictures should be valued by an expert. Get a bloke in from Sotheby's or the Dulwich Gallery to go over them before they end up on the walls of the Lees' lounge or get sold off for peanuts at some carboot or traded in for a tumble drier. Not to mention what the frames would fetch. And that's only the pictures, the house must be worth a bob or two with the way property prices are going, even though poor old John, bless him, hadn't touched it for years. Shame he wasn't as handy with the Dulux and Black and Decker as the old oilpaints."

"Still, she's not dead yet though, is she?" said Lisa.

"There's no need to be unpleasant," said Sonia.

Kevin, Rachel's husband, asked, "So what do you reckon to England's chances then?" but nobody answered.

"I think it's about time you paid your great aunt a visit, my son," Buster said to Nathan.

"My sentiments exactly." Nathan raised his glass to his father.

"I wonder if I can make room for a knickerbocker glory, Pat?" Sonia said, bringing her into the conversation.

"So, Nathan, you ever go to one of those sports bars up West?" asked Kevin.

"I have on occasion. Why?"

"I wouldn't mind going to one. Lads' night out, what do you say? You up for it, Richard, Sean? Ouch, what did I say now?" he rubbed his skin where Rachel had kicked him under the table.

Rachel couldn't bear the wistful way Kevin was looking up at Nathan, like a dog pleading for a walk.

"Yeah, all right then," said Nathan, wiping a heel of garlic bread round his plate. He couldn't stick it either. Sometimes he felt as if he were standing astride a river with his feet on boggy ground on either side. Soho on a Saturday night with tourists and lost souls from the burbs being sick in the gutter? Leicester Square? Live Sex Shows? No chance.

"I suppose you support Arsenal these days, Nathe, now you've deserted us for, Tufnell Park, is it?" said Uncle Leslie.

"That's right, only I'm seriously thinking of relocating to Hackney. Anyhow, I'll never desert the Eagles come what may."

"*Hackney?*" chorused Sonia and Pat.

"Will you sit still and behave!" Rachel turned miserably on her daughter who was gently tugging her sleeve.

"Oh, leave the child alone. She's all right, aren't you pet?" Sonia clucked at the embarrassed little girl. "Do you want the toilet, is that it? Come on, Nanny'll take you." She shot a look of triumph at Rachel.

"I'll take her. Come on, Amy."

"Somewhere round Hoxton Square. Everybody's out there now and there's some great studio spaces still going."

Rachel lifted Amy from her chair. Amy shrieked because the backs of her legs had stuck to the seat and she'd only been trying to ask for another milkshake because she wanted the paper parasol. She was the kind of child who collects up all the scraps off the Christmas crackers and hoards the foil from Easter eggs; her treasure trove would have made Nathan faint with envy. Rachel managed to hold back her own tears until they were in the Ladies, where she cried onto the top of Amy's head. Why did it always end up like this when Nathan was around? She and Kevin were making a real success of their little flower shop but he made them seem like nothing. The king of the castle sitting there holding court in a necklace of kids' sweets, jiggling his hairy thighs, making her look like a nagging wife. Dad had even handed him the wine list.

Later, at the coffee and liqueurs stage, when the tablecloth was blackened by the fallout from a dozen lighted amaretti papers and blobbed with red candlewax, Nathan caught and crushed the last ash parachute before it landed.

"You're looking very pensive, son," said Buster.

"Sorry, I was miles away. I was doing a few calculations in my head as to how I could raise the money for a computer. Something state-of-the-art, but it would have to be second-hand, sadly. You've got to have one nowadays, it's like an essential tool of the trade. If you're not on the Net you're dead."

"Leave it with me. You don't want to go messing around with second-hand rubbish. I'll make a few enquiries, see what I can come up with."

Buster slapped down a wad of notes, *Il padrone* tentatively presented each of the ladies with a red rose and Nathan scrawled his signature on the tablecloth.

"Don't go putting it into the washing machine, you've got a genuine bit of neo-post-abstract expressionism there. Hang on to it, mate. Better still, hang it on the wall. It'll keep you in pasta in your old age."

"I knew I shouldn't have had that knickerbocker glory," said Sonia. "I blame you, Pat."

CHAPTER THIRTEEN

At eight o'clock in the morning the back garden looked exhausted already in the sun that dazzled off every leaf and struck fool's gold from dry earth, and it was too late to water. The hose was heavy and dirty and she always had to dislodge a cluster of snails. Several gourds had fallen to the grass. Annoyed with herself for not having watered the night before, Lyris picked a few tomatoes whose cracked smiles were evidence of her erratic care and went inside as the doorbell rang.

It was Margaret the postwoman, with an envelope containing a book that was too big for the letterbox and a bundle of catalogues, cards and letters. Some years ago Lyris had purchased a skirt by mail order and now she was plagued by catalogues offering frumpy clothes at prohibitive prices. With no thought for the postman or the recipient who must dispose of them and their hateful shrinkwraps, ever spawning more, the catalogues pursued their campaign to take over the world. From time to time junk mail addressed to John made a surprise attack from out of the blue. Lyris chatted a while with Margaret and with a neighbor who was passing. She had known this girl in her pram and now she watched her guiding a little boy astride a tractor round the corner and out of sight.

Like Candy, Lyris had been concerned with a suitable birthday present for Isobel, who was not the easiest person to choose for. Besides, surely by the age of fifty a comfortably-off middle-class person had everything she might want and more, except perhaps a husband. She had decided to paint her a card, a signed original that Izzie need feel under no obligation to frame; that would kill two birds with one stone. Sorry, Izzie, just an expression, like "this won't get the baby a new frock." The response to that one had been tears over the telephone, and now Lyris paid a monthly direct debit to an orphanage in Romania. A hedgehog with fifty lighted candles for prickles? A bit risky. She settled for a watercolor of late summer flowers and fruits. But before she started she couldn't resist fiddling with the painting on the easel.

Time passed; an hour, two hours; she had no idea how long she had been there. She straightened her aching back. She had locked into an awkward position, sidesaddle on the old wooden donkey in the studio, staring into the overworked canvas, with two brushes sticking up from the back of her head like a Japanese hair ornament. The front doorbell rang. Zoe flashed into her mind and Lyris decided to ignore it. The bell rang again, its note prolonged by a bullying finger. Zoe or a pair of Jehovah's Witnesses.

"Go away, whoever you are!" she said under her breath.

The front door creaked open. Footsteps in the hall. Somebody was in her house. Lyris was motionless, a puppet jerked into an attitude of terror. Her throat constricted. A distant police car was yelping. Injury, shame and violation raced through her mind; she saw her wedding ring being wrenched from her finger, the gold studs ripped from her ears. Her slippery heart hurt as it leapt. A dark shape bulked in the studio doorway and she seized a large bottle of turpentine and flung it with all her strength but her arm was shaking so much, so enfeebled with fear, that it fell uselessly to the floor.

"That's a nice welcome I must say. You could've killed me, Auntie Lyris."

She was staring at him, bone-white, pressing a fist to her heart.

"I think you probably have killed me, Nathan."

She looked a hundred years old, with paintbrushes stuck in her hair, glasses slipping off her nose. He put down his bag and walked over to her.

"I'm really sorry. I didn't mean to scare you. I did ring the bell but the door was on the latch so I just came in. Here, have a drink of water."

He pressed a cup to her bloodless lips. She pushed it away.

"That's white spirit, you fool."

"I'll make you a cup of tea then. Look, I've said I was sorry, what more do you want? You might not be so lucky next time, leaving the door open like that. Anybody could just walk in. Still, no harm done, eh? I'll get the kettle on."

Lyris sat. She began to tremble. No harm done? Her heart thrashing about like a hooked fish; newsprint and television horrors coursing through her brain while she sat paralyzed, anticipating pain and even death; her body sprawled on the floor in a disorder of clothes. The garden hose, blocked by a snail, came into her mind as she recalled trying to force her voice through her throat, as in a nightmare when the scream can't get out. She pulled the paintbrushes from her hair and saw the wedding ring on her finger. The gold was worn thin by the years. It was impossible to slide it over the swollen joint.

She got up stiffly and followed Nathan into the kitchen.

"There you go. Nice cup of Rosie Lee, just what the doctor ordered. Hot and sweet. Sweet as a nut. You sit down and I'll bring it over. I'll just put these biscuits on a plate . . . big soggy for ginger-nuts, aren't they, never mind . . ."

Lyris watched Nathan bustling about like his mother and wondered what he was after. "They've been there since John died so it's no wonder they've lost something of their bite."

Nathan was relieved to see her acerbity return.

"That's more like it. You had me worried for a minute back there."

A flush of anger swept across Lyris's face.

"Yes, you've definitely got a bit of color back in your cheeks. I was thinking, I could fit a doorchain for you. Actually, I'm surprised your friend Tony hasn't insisted on doing it himself."

"Tony? How dare you suggest that Tony is in any way at fault? Anne and Tony have been like family. Besides, if you'd taken the trouble to look before bursting your way in, you'd have seen that there is a chain. It was my own carelessness in not closing the door properly."

Nathan spread out his hands in a self-deprecatory gesture. "All right, so I was out of order all along the way. I hold my hands up to it, but I've apologized so can we draw a line under it? I've been at home for a couple of days and Mum and Dad, they send their love by the way, were wondering how you were getting on. They've been meaning to come themselves, but you know how it is. So I said I'd pop in to say hello."

Like family. So the old man had been right, as usual.

Lyris was grateful that it was only Nathan sitting there and not Sonia and Buster, but was still suspicious. She noticed that the dreadful mustache was gone.

"That's very kind of them. Please give them my love and tell them that I'm keeping very well, and busy."

"Yeah? What are you busy doing? Anything in particular?"

She did look better now, less like some flaky pensioner and more like herself in her big yellow shirt over black pants and espa-drilles.

"And Lisa and Rachel? Is all well with them?"

"Yeah, they're fine. Same old same old, you know those two."

"I've always wished I had a sister."

"Have you?" Bit late now, he thought, she'd be an old woman. "So what've you been up to?"

Lyris bristled at the impertinence. "Why did you decide to take up art, Nathan?"

Nathan shifted in his chair. He scratched a tiny pustule like a droplet of varnish from his chin. "Well—lots of reasons. Why does any artist? To express himself I suppose. Much the same as you did probably."

"Which part of yourself is it that you want to express?"

"Well, you know. My feelings, myself, my take on the world . . ."

"And you felt that paint was the medium through which you could best do this?"

"Yes. I mean, no, not entirely. Paint as such doesn't interest me that much, it's too limited. You know most of my stuff is conceptual. Anyhow I'm really into computer-generated images now."

"But Hockney did that years ago."

The words "old hat" skimmed across the kitchen.

"I'm not talking pretty pictures here, I'm talking cyberspace—what is this anyway, the third degree?"

What did he have to do to impress her? Paint some bleeding flowers in a jug?

Reminded that he'd just scraped a Third, Lyris said, "I'm only trying to get in touch with the *Zeitgeist*. To feel the cutting edge. Everything's remixed and recycled nowadays and I want to be able to take the references in some multi-media project. After all, Nathan, I've lived through a number of movements and I'd like to understand what your generation is up to. I've done many things in my time, woodcuts, lithographs, sculpture, pottery, but for me it's always really been painting, always as much about the paint itself as the image. After all these years I still get excited about the possibilities of paint."

Uncertain if he was being got at, Nathan refilled their mugs.

He had found printmaking really boring. A scraperboard set Lyris had given him one birthday came into his mind. It had been confiscated after he'd stabbed Lisa in the leg with one of the tools.

"You'll have to come to my new studio once I've relocated to Hoxton. One piece in particular I think you'd appreciate. I feel as if I've moved on from the group I was involved with. Plus, as I say, I'm doing a lot on the Web. Shame you're not on the Net or you could log on to it. By the way, a friend of mine asked for your address the other night. Zoe? I wondered if she'd been in touch yet?"

"Oh yes. Your friend Zoe has been in touch. In fact, she's been here."

"She has? Fantastic. You don't happen to have her number do you, or her address? Only I seem to have mislaid it."

So that's it, though Lyris.

"I may have her card somewhere. Oh dear, I do hope I didn't throw it away."

"Could you have a look? Please. It's really important. Tell me where it might be and I'll have a look for it."

Nathan jumped up and began searching, riffling through cards from people who had been at John's retrospective and the bunch of invitations behind the vase. Then the shelf of cookery books stuffed with brittle recipes cut from newspapers and magazines.

"This reminds me of Hunt the Thimble when you children were small. Remember? You're getting colder . . ." she sang out as he approached the fridge.

"Come on, don't tease. Gimme a break, willya. Is it even in this room?"

"Funnily enough, Zoe is anxious to get in touch with you, too."

"No! Really? Did she say that? What did she say, exactly?"

"Something about a film, I think it was . . ."

"A film? She wants me to go to the pictures with her?"

"A film she intends to make."

"Make? She wants to make a film about me?"

"No. About me."

Lyris relented and gave Nathan Zoe's card.

"Mind if I use your phone? I suppose I'd better give her a ring."

Nathan returned looking crestfallen.

"I had to leave a message on her machine. I ought to be going, in case she calls me back at home. I'm going to have to get myself a mobile."

Watching Nathan become vulnerable and boyish, obviously in love with the dreadful Zoe, Lyris warmed to him. There was a question on the tip of her tongue but she kept forgetting what it was. She supposed she ought to tell him that she had no intention of participating in any film but decided to leave it for the moment.

"Won't you stay and have a bit of lunch? After all, if she's out on a shoot somewhere she probably won't be back for ages."

Nathan remembered that he had come also to check out her art collection and to prove himself worthy of inheriting it.

"Yeah, all right then. I'd like that. Thanks."

The telephone rang. Nathan moved to answer it. "That was quick! She must be keen."

"I'll get it. There's just the faintest chance that it might be for me."

Nathan walked round the kitchen in a daze. There he was, thinking he'd blown it with Zoe and all the time she wanted to put him in a film. Double whammy. A chance to get to know Zoe and a showcase for his work. It just went to prove that he had to have more belief in himself.

"Who was it?"

"Just somebody for me. The world doesn't revolve around you, you know."

"Why have you got it in for me? I used to think you liked me when I was a little boy. All that magic painting and stuff. I've still got the stegosaurus we made on this kitchen table after we went to the Natural History Museum."

"Oh Nathan, I do like you. That's why I—care. That's why I mind when you exhibit a photocopy of your bottom at your degree show and think that it will do."

"You seriously missed the point there. It was an ironic comment on the fundamental sadness of the bloke who sits on the photocopier at the office party."

"I apologize then."

He had never forgotten that first visit to the Natural History Museum where the albino birds and animals, the arctic hares and foxes frozen in their glass cages, fascinated him even more than the gigantic skeletons.

He pointed to a winter landscape on the wall, black crows in a wild sky above a furrowed field. "That's nice. Who is it? Nash?"

"No, it's one of mine."

"Oh yes, you're right. I'll have to reacquaint myself with your collection whilst I'm here. You don't always appreciate things when you're younger, do you? And I'd love to see your recent stuff—what was that on the easel, a still life?"

"No. It's not really working. It's gone over. It's called "The Blue Bead". I was preoccupied with the question of how long a prisoner in isolation say, or subjected to a degrading regime designed to break, to take everything away, can retain a sense of self. Or an orphaned refugee child with no memories, with nothing from its past but perhaps a single blue bead to show it once had an identity. The implications of that phrase "a displaced person". It's about the terrible poignancy of our possessions and how they define and console us."

"Funnily enough, I've been thinking a lot about prison myself. Art in prisons."

"How extraordinary!"

Lyris was jolted by this new perspective on Nathan and felt that she had been too quick to judge and dismiss him as shallow and self-obsessed. As he had said, he needn't have come to see her.

"And the War. All those VE Day celebrations got me interested," he was saying.

She told him a little about her and John's experiences as War Artists and asked if he had seen their paintings in the gallery at the Imperial War Museum.

"I went with the school years ago. I was going to go to The Blitz Experience but I missed it, as you do. I didn't know they had a gallery, I'll have to check it out."

"Yes do. You'll find some Nashes and there are a couple of lovely Rodrigo Moynihan portraits."

"Right. Could be useful."

"I will indeed visit your studio to see your new work. I haven't got anything very exciting for lunch, I'm afraid. Would some macaroni do, with runner beans? Or salad and bread and cheese as it's so hot?"

"Whatever. I know it will be delicious. You always were a terrific cook."

They ate in the garden. Lyris had given Nathan a bottle of wine to open. He raised his glass in a toast, looking at her and wondering what he'd be like when he was old. He saw himself sitting in her place in a linen jacket and panama hat. Lyris had uncoiled the hose for later; somehow it was so much easier to do things when there was somebody else there, as if an observer provided motivation and gave the action a reality it lacked when one was alone.

"You ought to get yourself a sprinkler," said Nathan. "Mum's got hers going non-stop at the moment."

Of course she has, thought Lyris contentedly. Sprinkler bans are for the little people. Nathan had eaten most of their lunch. She was gratified that he enjoyed it, and she was dining with friends. Their cigarette smoke spiralled blue on blue.

"Are these things just ornamental or can you eat them?" asked Nathan, picking up a gourd and weighing it in his hand. "Some of them are a bit suggestive. They're a bit rude, aren't they?"

"Don't be so solipsistic. We're all part of nature so it's only reasonable that we should look alike in some respects."

They talked more that afternoon than in all the preceding years. When they disagreed, the bitterness had gone out of their exchanges.

"Soho's so unpleasant these days. It's really gone to the dogs," Lyris said at one point.

"You mean it's not full of sad old gits boring on about the glory days when Muriel kicked them down the stairs and boozy old tarts who were anybody's for the price of a gin."

Lyris laughed.

"Anyway, Lyris, you've got to see it in a historical context. You say Soho has gone to the dogs but it was named after an old hunting cry, wasn't it? So-ho! So-ho! Yoicks! Tally ho! What do you think those old huntsmen would've made of your lot?"

He was lying on his back. The top of his head looked like a fuzzy tangerine. She resisted an impulse to stroke it. His feet were bare. Lyris had a flashback of his figure blocking the doorway to the studio. Why did one so fear the feet and legs of the intruder? Too many films showing the toes of a pair of shoes beneath a heavy curtain.

"Do you want those snails?" he asked. "I've got an idea of how I could use them."

"Mmm, I do rather," Lyris lied, imagining a befouled tank in some cruel installation. "They seek the moisture of the hose, you see. They're very clever. Some of them have sealed themselves into their shells to survive the drought."

"I see," said Nathan, who didn't. How clever could snails be? Could they be taught to do performance art?

"I've begun to long for rain myself. Real rain, not just an isolated downpour. I come out here and I feel like a wildebeeste sniffing the air and pawing the veldt."

"You know what you were saying earlier, about why did I decide to take up art? I was too embarrassed to say before but it's all down to you, you know. Remember one half-term when I was about thirteen and you took me to the British Museum and we went into Cornelisson's on the way? Mum must have dumped me on you to keep me out of mischief. I was throwing a right old moody, expecting to be bored shitless by the whole expedition. And then suddenly I looked around the shop and there were all these jars of brilliant colored pigments and crystals with names that I couldn't hardly read, drawers full of crayons and chalks and big fat pastels. It was magic. Like being in an alchemist's laboratory. The brushes, the inks, the colored papers, the touch, the smell, I wanted the lot."

Lyris reached for his hand and pressed it without saying anything. Her eyes filled with tears.

"So you see, Great Aunt Lyris, I owe it all to you. Otherwise I'd be minding a flower stall somewhere in South London, mixed up in all sorts and keeping one eye open for the cozzers; wife, kids and mortgage round my neck."

"Cozzers?"

"The Old Bill. The police."

"Oh. I thought they must be some kind of flowers, like mums or daffs. A sort of cosmos. I'll take a bunch of mixed cozzers with a bit of gyp. By the way, have you seen the Seurat show yet?"

"Nah. Didn't see the point."

As Lyris washed up after Nathan had left, with half a dozen gourds tucked into his clean washing, she whistled softly, something she did unconsciously when she was happy; potato, potahto, tomayto, tomato, let's call the calling off off. A vague memory surfaced, of Nathan pulling out drawers and fingering things in Cornelisson's, of buying him a drawing book, and apologizing and paying for a rubber he had slipped into his pocket.

"Don't forget your burgling bag," she had joked as he kissed her goodbye. Nathan's boredom threshold was perceptively higher and she found herself wishing that John could witness his graceless protégé's blossoming, and feel vindicated for having pleaded his cause at Chelsea. Of course, Buster had leaned on John fairly heavily. When they came to a rectangle of pale wall exposed by the removal of one of John's paintings Nathan had asked how the sales were going.

"I haven't the faintest idea. Louis hasn't been in touch at all."

"Leave it with me. I'll sort him out."

Nathan had revealed enormous *lacunae* in the course of their discussions, but perhaps they weren't entirely the boy's fault. He confessed that he had been to the National Gallery only a few times since John had dragged him round before his interview. As far as the permanent collection went, he quite liked the Impressionists, but he was put off by not having a clue what all those mythological paintings were supposed to be about. They reminded him of church and he hated churches, not that he'd been inside one since he'd left the Cubs except for weddings.

"You have no interest even in their architecture? But Nathan, to understand how painting has arrived where it is today, you have to look at the past! You're missing so much and apart from that you're shutting yourself off from all that alchemy you mentioned. It isn't just subject matter, it's history and politics and chemistry. It's about how developments in science and industry have given artists the range and freedom to work as they do now."

They had agreed to visit the Seurat exhibition at the National Gallery together and she was going to take him to lunch at the Tate, but their first outing was to be to the Dulwich Picture Gallery. Their first date. Lyris smiled at the incongruity. Nathan was by no means a *tabula rasa*, indeed quite a lot of graffiti were scrawled over him, but it would be fun. As for books, it seemed that his taste ran entirely to the neo-Gothic. She began to compile a reading list in her head. What a strange mixture of a boy he was. Yes, it was fun to have somebody to care about again.

She must try not to be so bossy next time although she looked forward to sharing things with him. They would make a change from the usual art gallery scenario where a pompous man pontificates to his hapless female companion, but she could learn from Nathan too. The mysteries of the new technology. Drying her hands, she remembered what she had meant to ask him: what's become of Jackee? All she could recall of her now was her Medusa head. There were a few things she needed from the shops and she got herself ready to go out. When she went to pick up her purse from the kitchen table, it was gone.

CHAPTER FOURTEEN

Seb was cowering in a corner holding up a canvas like a shield to ward off a furious blue-and-white-striped tigress. She whirled round as Nathan came into the studio.

"Perhaps I can get some sense out of you!"

"I can explain—I never even knew I had it—"

Then he realised she was Josh's mother and not a policewoman.

"What do you mean?" he asked.

"My son! Josh! Where the hell is he? Has he been with you?"

"No. How should I know where he is? Why?"

"He seems to have gone missing," said Seb, putting down his shield.

"Seems to have! He *has* gone missing! I haven't heard from him for days and he's not at his flat. You must know something!"

She was terrifying, in a butcher's striped shirt with the collar turned up, belted into jeans; long slim legs, blue wedgie espadrilles with a glimpse of red toenail. Sunglasses on the top of her head pulling the gilded hair off her forehead, big pearl earrings, flawless makeup.

"Stop staring at me like a cretin. I want to know what's happened to my son!"

"I don't know. Haven't clapped eyes on him for days. I've been away myself, staying at my parents'. How do you know he hasn't just gone off on some project? He doesn't ring you every day, does he?"

"Of course he does. I'm his mother."

Seb and Nathan exchanged a look.

"So you've been with your folks then?" said Seb.

"I've tried the police, the hospitals. Nobody seems to give a damn."

"Here, don't upset yourself. You sit down and I'll make you a nice cup of Rosie—a cup of tea."

"I don't want your stinking tea, or your *faux* cockney solicitude. I want my son."

She did sit down, sweeping a pile of drawings off a crate.

"Look, I'm sure he's all right. He's a big boy now."

Josh's mother blew her nose. "It's all my fault. I was the one who encouraged him to do his own thing, get all this art nonsense out of his system. If he'd followed his father into the army none of this would have happened."

"Except that he might be dead of course. Got himself killed, I mean," said Nathan.

"How dare you! I should never have let him get mixed up with people like you—degenerates, scroungers, barrow-boys! I know all about you and your drugs. If anything's happened to Josh I shall hold you personally responsible."

She took her diary from her bag, wrote on a page, ripped it out and thrust it at Seb.

"This is my number. Call me at once if you hear anything at all, do you hear? Night or day."

"Hey, it's not our fault—" Seb began as she stood up.

"You're his friends. You should have looked after him."

She stalked out.

"Talk about going for the jugular," said Nathan.

"I know. Thank God you came in when you did. She was just about to rip my throat out."

"I meant calling me a barrow-boy. I shouldn't have let her get away with it, insulting my parents like that."

He walked over to the window as an engine started up.

"Look at that! Fucking 4WD, wouldn't you know it. Fucking Shogun! Just what you need for getting around rural Chelsea. Wheels right across the fucking pavement and I bet she didn't even get a fucking ticket. I hate people like that. Think they own the whole fucking world."

"Mothers!" said Seb. "Makes me realize how lucky I was mine ran off to Argentina when she did, on my seventh birthday."

"What about the others, don't they know where Josh is?"

"They're out looking for him now. Mummy had Howard in tears. How's Fatima then?"

"Zoe. Her name's Zoe. Fatima was just a joke. She's fine. We're doing a film together."

The emotions that crossed Seb's face did nothing for Nathan. There was a weight on his heart in the shape of a velvet purse.

"I'd better get going, she's ringing me at home. We'll have to get an answerphone for this place."

"What about Josh?"

"What about him?"

"Hang on a minute, Nathan, there's something I want to talk to you about. Strictly between ourselves, OK? Don't take this the wrong way, but I've given it a lot of thought. I wouldn't want you to think I was being disloyal or underhand . . ."

"Get on with it, man. I'm in a hurry. You want me out of the Group, right? Fine. Suits me. Don't give it another thought. I don't need any of you."

"No. You've got it all wrong. I was thinking, Gilbert and

George, Barker and Tooze, The Chapman Brothers. Duos. You and me, what do you say? Seb and Nathan."

Nathan stared at him. Then he said,

"You're a shit, Seb. You know that?"

And walked out.

Every conceivable explanation whirled round in Lyris's mind but they all came back to the hideous starting-place. Nathan had stolen her purse. It was no use trying to convince herself that he might have picked it up accidentally; even so she had waited for him to come running back, full of apologies. When it became obvious that he wasn't going to, her ears strained towards the telephone, willing it to ring with a torrent of embarrassed excuses: he had just found her purse in his bag—he'd no idea how it got there. It must have fallen in somehow, maybe it got swept up with the gourds. She heard the conversation in her head: "No, don't bother to post it. There was hardly anything in it but I'm rather fond of it. Just bring it with you on Sunday."

In her mind's eye she could see the purse lying on the kitchen table yet she looked in her bedroom, even in the bathroom where she saw that the seat had been left up. She searched the studio, feeling down the sides of the chair, looking under piles of sketchbooks that hadn't been touched for years, behind canvases disturbed by Zoe. She sat down on the donkey struck by a ray of hope. It was quite possible that Nathan had not opened his bag yet. Might not open it for days. Should she telephone him? No, that would look like an accusation, and she couldn't face it, or the possibility of lies. Perhaps she herself had slipped the purse into his bag, like Pharaoh hiding his precious cup in Benjamin's sack? What nonsense. Besides, Nathan couldn't distinguish Pharaoh from Bacchus. He was an ignorant lout who had broken into her house and after playing her for a sucker, letting her ramble on like a gullible old fool, he had taken what he'd come for. He was from a criminal family. That black bag was probably full of housebreaking tools. How he must have sniggered on the train. Then cursed her when he realized how little money the purse contained. A few notes, a few coins and no credit cards. She supposed he threw it out of the window.

Once scarlet and magenta with embroidered flowers, the purse was now balding and floppy. It was only a bit of old velvet with a zip, lying on the clinker beside a railway track. It was only a thing. And Nathan was only a boy whom she had thought she could love. So much for the blue bead of memory. So much for the poignancy of possessions. What did she presume to know of brutality anyway? She slashed ultramarine across the khaki mud of the canvas.

Zoe was wearing a white vest that left little to Nathan's imagination and a skirt so short that he caught a flash of her tiny boxer shorts when she crossed and uncrossed her legs; underwear like his own but smaller and whiter. They were sitting on a bench at one of the tables in the courtyard outside the pub off the Portobello Road where Zoe had instructed Nathan to meet her. It was crowded outside and in. Nathan had been late and only Zoe's willpower and her intimidatingly long legs sprawled along the seat had enabled her to reserve a place for him.

"Am I boring you?" asked Zoe.

"No. Why?"

"It's like you don't want to be here. It's like you're a different person from the one you were the other night. Is it something I said?"

"No. Go on about the film. I'm really interested. Over the moon," he added, gazing miserably into the evening sky.

"Every time I mention Lyris you clam up and get a glazed look in your eyes."

"It's her I'm worried about," he blurted out. "Lyris. I probably shouldn't say this, but I thinks she's losing it a bit. I've just spent the afternoon with her and she—well, for starters she'd left the front door wide open. Anybody could've walked in off the street."

"But they didn't, did they?"

"She shouldn't be on her own."

"Well she won't be, with a film crew all over the place, will she? Do you want to get us another?"

She had been playing with a five-pound note but she didn't offer it to Nathan. As Nathan lumbered inside through the drinkers, Zoe looked at her watch. If she was prepared to forget Nathan's behavior after the party, his grabbing her and shoving his tongue down her throat, the least he could do was be grateful. She rolled the fiver into a thin tube, took a nail-file and compact from her bag and opened it on her thigh under the table, bent her head and sniffed.

Nathan was jostled at the bar by girls who were younger versions of Josh's mother, demanding mescal with a worm. He felt short and grungy. Everybody else seemed to be having a good time. Here he was, with the girl of his fantasies on a hot evening, with the prospect of being in a film, and he was acting like a prat. All because of a stupid purse. It was pathetic. The worst thing was, he didn't even know why he'd taken it. Later, after they'd got talking, he'd decided to put it back. Then he'd forgotten all about it. His heart had stopped when he had pulled it out of his pocket on the train. He couldn't decide if it would be better to ring Lyris, he could do it from here, and say he'd found it in his bag, or to pretend he knew nothing about it. If Lyris said anything he could suggest that somebody had got in and nicked it before he'd arrived.

"What's this?" said Zoe when he put down their drinks.

"V and T."

"I asked for an Absolut Sea Breeze."

"Sorry. I've got a lot on my mind."

"Don't worry, I'll have this one."

A sunburnt male hand reached past Nathan and poured tonic into the glass.

"What's your game?" Nathan raised his fist, and dropped it as the bloke kissed the top of Zoe's head, saying, "Sorry I'm late, sweetheart. Phew, what a scorcher."

He ran his finger down her arched throat to her glistening cleavage then held out his hand to Nathan.

"Dan. You must be Nathan."

He was about six feet tall, cropped black hair, white T-shirt sleeves rolled over the curves of his biceps.

"What are you drinking?" he said.

He picked up Nathan's beer and looked at the label.

"I'll join you. And, Nat, that's an Absolut Sea Breeze, OK?"

Nathan stood, seething with black disbelief and disappointment. They had their heads together now, whispering. As if he was the waiter. Well they could wait.

He bought himself a beer and brooded over it at a corner of the bar. He ought to be out of here. The thought of Zoe and Dan sickened him. The way he'd touched her like that, making their relationship obvious for his benefit. They were probably laughing at him now for thinking he was in with a chance. But if he were to walk out now he could kiss the film goodbye, and he'd have to face Seb. No girlfriend, no film. Seb was turning into the old man of the sea, dragging him down. Seb and Nathan. Nathan and Seb. It sounded like some failed comedy act or a pair of one-hit wonders. If Lyris was to tell Zoe about the purse he was dead anyway. Nathan Pursey the artist branded a common thief, a tea leaf who robbed old ladies. If he walked out now she'd take it as proof of his guilt. Nathan finished his beer and ordered two more and an Absolut Sea Breeze. On his way back he took a glug from one of the beers, washed it round his mouth and back into the bottle.

"There you are," said Dan lazily. "We were just about to send out a search party."

"Sorry about that. Had to call my dealer back. My art dealer, I should say in this instance. Cheers!"

He watched as Dan tilted back the bottle he had spat in.

"So, Zoe. Where were we as regards the film?"

At the same time, at her friends' house in Dulwich, Lyris took a sip of white wine and shivered as she remembered Nathan trying to force white spirit past her lips.

CHAPTER FIFTEEN

Candy was behind the counter of Criterion Cleaners, helping out while Belinda the regular girl took her little boy to the doctor's. They had the front and back doors open but it was still almost intolerably hot. Candy enjoyed working there. She got a buzz from being needed; she liked clipping on a pair of workaday earrings, lacing up her white high-heeled sneakers and buttoning the short white coat that made her feel efficient and vaguely medical. Today anything more than her underwear, which showed when she stood against the light, beneath the white coat would have been unthinkable. It gave her pleasure to gather up some creased garment, perhaps with a difficult or embarrassing stain, from a shamefaced customer and return it to its owner all fresh and pressed with pristine triangles of tissue pinned under its shoulders. If only clothes could speak, she often thought, what tales they could tell, but it was probably just as well they couldn't. Most of all she loved presenting a secondhand wedding dress restored to virginal whiteness to a blushing bride, even if she felt a little sad once the girl had left the shop. Billy the manager came through the bead curtain that concealed the machines, wiping his face and saying,

"It's a rainforest out there. All we need is a few Amazon parrots flying around."

For a moment it seemed a lovely idea to Candy. Then she

considered a budgie but supposed it might die in the fumes like a canary down a mine.

"I'll go next door and get us some iced tea," she said.

She ignored a wolf-whistle from a workman on a roof with a disdainful toss of her head. The first she'd heard for ages, she realized. Obviously the message had got through that it was unacceptable. Or was it that nobody wolf-whistled her any more?

When she came back Billy was dabbing his lower eyelid with the corner of a tissue.

"This humidity wreaks havoc. I thought this mascara was supposed to be waterproof."

"I'll lend you mine. It's tried and tested."

"Has he been in touch?"

She shook her head.

"I thought not. We haven't seen your red satin bustier in here for quite a while, have we?"

They stirred their iced tea.

"Never mind. You'd be better off with Clovis, I always think. Belinda was only saying yesterday, 'I wonder why those two don't get it together'."

"Oh, Clovis is just a friend. We're buddies, that's all. But funnily enough, he *has* invited me to go to his ex-wife's birthday party with him."

"Trying to make her jealous, I suppose."

"Oh, I don't think so. I think he genuinely wants my company."

Candy felt deflated. The last thing she needed was to be caught up in somebody else's emotional drama. To be used. She changed the subject.

"How's the book coming on?"

Billy was writing a novel, *Bring On the Empty Coathangers*. He agreed with Candy that every garment told a story and his author reading at Criterion Books had been on Clovis's schedule for several years now.

"Getting there. They say everybody's got a book in them but they don't tell you how hard it is to get it out. Probably take a Caesarian in my case. Now, if anybody should write their memoirs, it should be you, Candy. Fame and fortune, serialization in the Sundays, breakfast television . . ."

"I don't think anybody would be that interested now. And not in my life anyway."

"You're too modest. I hope you're wrong because I've put you in my book."

"You wouldn't! You haven't? You're winding me up, aren't you? You wouldn't do that to me?"

"I thought you'd be pleased. There's no need to look so horrified, your secrets are safe with me. Nobody will recognise you—I've called you Cindy."

Billy went through to the back. Candy picked up a refill for an Eazi-Clean clothes brush, a roll of sticky tape on a handle, and picked at the edge. It was just a glorified version of those horrible flypapers people used to have when she was a child. She always kept an Eazi-Clean handy at home and it had proved invaluable for removing dog hairs from Rayner's suits. He would think she had betrayed him utterly when Billy's book came out—and she supposed she had. She could only pray that Billy never finished it; or perhaps one of the machines might overheat and the shop catch fire, destroying the manuscript. She could hear that Billy was upset from the way he was shrugging the plastic over the pressed clothes. A customer came in and Candy served her with a bright little smile masking her growing fears that all the time she had been working at Criterion Cleaners Billy had just been using her as material, preparing to wash her dirty linen in public.

By the time the customer and the man who followed her had gone, Candy had put herself in the wrong, as was her habit. Billy's partner had died two years previously and his writing was all that kept him going. He'd probably risk his life trying to save his manuscript from the flames, could even die in the attempt. Candy recalled him saying once that he'd intended to end his days on the Hoffmann Press. She put her arms round him and said she was highly flattered to be in his novel and couldn't wait to read it.

"You've really got to let go, you know. He's not coming back. The relationship's toast and everybody but you can see it. It's time you got on with your life," he told her.

My life? thought Candy. I wish he wouldn't keep going on about my life. What is my life? Where has it all gone? She had been cheated somehow while she hardly noticed. She reckoned she was entitled to claim back quite a large rebate in years she hadn't lived.

"So what do you think I should get for Clovis's ex's birthday? It's her fiftieth. He's asked me to choose something from us both."

"What's she like? What are her interests?"

"Well, she's very into animals, animal welfare. She likes dogs. And she's a magistrate."

"A gift-wrapped veal calf in its own crate? A Rottweiler? Handcuffs?"

"I don't think so. But you've given me an idea."

After they had closed for the day Candy dropped in on Clovis to see if he fancied a walk in the park but he turned her down, saying he had to get changed to go out to a ridiculous dinner party.

"Just thought I'd ask," she said cheerfully.

Why don't I ever go to dinner parties? she wondered. She went home to shower and change into shorts, a pink halterneck T-shirt and denim cowboy boots before harnessing the dogs. People assumed because of their size that they were all pups, but really some of them were quite elderly doggies now. Candy monitored Sherpa's back legs as they trotted along. She might have to consider some alternative means of transport eventually—perhaps one of those old-fashioned prams, or skateboards or a small cart pulled by the fittest dogs. Then she saw, in an unhappy flash, how easily a glamorous person in charge of an amusing invention could be mistaken for a batty old woman with too many dogs.

She sat on a bench and, resolving not to let her guard slip for a moment, took her lipstick from the pocket of her shorts. She would not allow anybody, not even herself, to see that she cared that Rayner had dumped her or that she missed him. She was not the sort to go whining that he had robbed her of the best years of her life. After all, it takes two to tango. Plenty more fish in the sea besides that great floundering cod. She lit a cigarette, scattered a cloud of midges with a small tornado of smoke, and looked up into the branches of the cedar and saw pale green cones sitting like gift soaps among the needles. You could almost feel their silky, sculpted surface as you lifted them out of the green box and sniffed their fragrance. Candy did sniff, at a sudden prickle of tears.

"Come on, little guys, home!"

She cracked the leads like a whip against her boot.

Candy's face had been her fortune. If she had not been such a pretty child, just a shade less blonde, with slightly paler and smaller blue eyes, she might not have been going home now to an empty flat full of the presents Rayner had given her over the years. An unfortunate nose or stubbier legs might have saved her later. As it was, she had been a mail order catalogue model at four, the carnival queen of Cambury at fifteen. Candy had never known her father and her mother had died soon after her only daughter's triumphal procession through the town on a decorated float with balloons and streamers waving. She had a white dress with a sash across her shoulder and a tiara in her hair. The nurses had wheeled her mother to the hospital gate and Candy threw her bouquet to her like a bride and her mother caught it.

The council regretted that Candy was too young to take over the tenancy of the house where she had grown up; she had no relatives that she knew of, and nobody knew what to do about her. Candy solved their problems for them by taking the train to London. As she sat on a bench at Paddington Station, eating a bar of chocolate and not knowing whether to look first at the accommodation to let or the situations vacant in the *Evening News*, a man in sunglasses sat down beside her and began to chat.

"I'm Carl. What's your name?" he asked her. "Candy? That's sweet. Like you."

Candy was not entirely surprised when Carl said he repre-sented a model agency; he was so good-looking and sophisticated. This was what she expected life in London to be like, and she *was* the carnival queen of Cambury. She picked up her suitcase containing her clothes, a few mementoes of her mother, two dolls and a teddy bear, and went with him. It was her first ride in a London taxi. If only Mum could see me now, she thought, as the cab carried them the short distance to the heart of the Rachman empire.

CHAPTER SIXTEEN

Clovis had arrived in a bad mood and was finding the dinner party very tedious. It was at the Highgate house of Jenny and Christopher who wrote and illustrated children's books; they were inveterate collectors of ephemera and every room was full of gewgaws, tin clockwork toys and automata for guests to play with. Clovis was fond of them but tonight was mildly irritated by everything about them: their ingenuous kindness, Jenny's kaftan, their amusing house, the ceiling fan that pushed the air around. Seated between Jenny and a girl to whom he had taken an instant dislike, who kept flicking back her hair, Clovis drank more than usual hoping it would make him more affable. From time to time the computer bore opposite kicked him in an attempt to make contact with the annoying girl's leg. Her lips were too glossy, her hair too shiny, everything about her, including her dress, was slippery. She was an eel slithering about on her chair, forking cold fish into her mouth. Clovis made an effort and asked if she lived nearby. The nerd answered for her.

"No, we're south of the river now. *Sarf* London. We're *Sarf* Londoners, ain't we, babes?"

"Yeah, *Sarf* Londoners, innit," she squeaked.

"Arf arf arf," said Clovis.

Jenny and Christopher exchanged a look. Clovis was usually

so reliable and here he was barking like a dog. Joke over, the young man explained rather stiffly that it was Dulwich, actually.

"Didn't Maggie buy a house there, Rod?" Christopher asked.

"I believe she did. On one of the estates, but she never moved in. Apparently the place was like a fortress."

"Say what you like about her," the slippery girl said, "but you've got to hand it to her . . ."

"At least she—" Rod began, and the dinner party was back on track, until Clovis derailed it by saying,

"No she didn't."

"Didn't what?"

"Make the trains run on time."

"That's not what I was going to say. Have you got a problem with something?"

"No. No, I apologize. Please go on with what you were saying."

Rod did. There were eight of them round the table. Jenny and Christopher, Sidney Leeds the septuagenarian poet and his latest girlfriend Lucinda, whom nobody had met before this evening, who had allergies and had brought her own food in a Postman Pat lunchbox, Gita Shah, a novelist whom Clovis had known for years, and the young couple Rod and Nancy. Lucinda wound up a clock-work mouse and set it running over the tablecloth but everybody else was in tacit agreement to ignore it.

Plus ça change, thought Clovis. Here we all are, sitting over dinner talking about Mrs. Thatcher. It was not until Christopher asked, "And what does Rayner have to say about the show so far, Nancy? Finding it a bit hard to adjust, I expect," that Clovis realized who she was. Small bloody world. Talk about six degrees of separation. He turned to her.

"So you're Nancy *Carmody? Rayner* Carmody's daughter."

Little Nancy who had ridden her pony over Candy's foot fledged into a publicity girl.

"Yes. Do you know Daddy?"

"Yes I do, as a matter of fact. I know him rather well. I've known him for years."

"S'traordinary. I was at school with Rayner," said Christopher. "I'd no idea."

"Small world," Nancy was saying. "Actually, Christopher, Daddy's been incredible and it's lovely for Mummy to have him to herself again. He's doing some consultancy work and various things of course but he's like a—"

"Pig in shi—clover," supplied Clovis.

"Would you mind repeating that?" Rod pushed back his chair and leaned across the table, thrusting his face at Clovis.

"Now, Rod, I'm sure Clovis didn't mean—" Jenny reached over to clutch Rod's arm, knocking over a glass of red wine that poured into the lap of his chinos.

"Bloody hell!"

"Oh, Rod, I'm so sorry. Quick, soak it up with your napkin!"

"Salt," ordered Sidney Leeds.

"No, pour some white wine on it," said Lucinda.

"Cold water's the only thing that works."

How relieved everybody was at the diversion. It gave Lucinda a chance to contribute to the conversation.

"Come with me, Rod, I'll sort you out." Christopher led him away.

"I'll be sending you the cleaning bill," Rod threatened Clovis over his shoulder. "And not just for the trousers. It's gone right through to my Calvins."

"Oh, poor you. Yes, do. I insist. I do feel rather to blame. In fact, if you give me the pants, and the Calvins, I'll have them done myself. I've got a marvelous little woman—she's a trifle lame in one fetlock but I wouldn't trust anybody else with my knickers."

"Clovis, have you gone mad?" Gita hissed. "You're completely wrecking Jenny's party."

"Very few people look good in chinos, have you noticed, Lucinda?" Clovis said. "Something about the cut, the way they pouch. Most unflattering."

"Are you gay?"

"No, I'm an aesthete."

He sipped the mineral water which Gita had poured loudly into his glass and turned to Nancy. Her eyes were full of tears and a strand of hair had stuck to her lipgloss. He held her happiness and Rayner's future in his hand. How would Miranda feel if some malevolent stranger exposed him as an old goat at a dinner party? He had a flashback of the slumped figure on the escalator and became conscious of a lurking unhappy awareness that he hadn't telephoned Miranda for some time. He would find an amusing postcard for her in the morning.

"I do apologize. A most unfortunate misunderstanding. I meant only that it must be a relief for Rayner to have exchanged the hurly-burly of the division bell for life on the farm. So you're in publishing? Anything exciting happening there?"

"Actually, I've got the most horrendous author arriving from Singapore tomorrow. A real prima donna. Apparently he's mega out there but nobody's heard of him here and I haven't been able to fix up a single interview or reading. I'm picking him up at the airport and he's going to go absolutely ballistic. I know it's a cheek but I'm desperate. You've got a bookshop, haven't you? I don't suppose . . ."

"Out of the question," said Clovis firmly.

"What a wonderful idea!" "Perfect!" exclaimed Jenny and Gita.

"Probably have you flogged or beheaded. Isn't that what they do out there?" chuckled Sidney Leeds.

"Pretty please," Nancy simpered, hardening Clovis's heart.

"I'd help you out if I could, but it's a tiny shop and I've just taken in more stock. There really isn't the space for an audience."

"All the better."

"I didn't know you had readings in your shop. How very interesting," said Sidney Leeds. People always referred to him by his full name, perhaps because they didn't like him much.

Christopher and Rod, in a pair of Christopher's trousers, returned as Jenny carried in the summer pudding, her speciality which she made in a child's seaside bucket shaped like a castle. There was cigarette smoke in the air. Everybody was chatting away as if the dinner party had gelled at last. Except Clovis, who was looking a bit green round the gills.

"Can't I tempt you, Lucinda? Just a spoonful?" Jenny coaxed.

"No, I'm all right, thanks. I've got a Frusli bar."

CHAPTER SEVENTEEN

Anne was woken from a deep sleep by hail hitting the bedroom window and bombarding the sills and gutters. She lay, with Tony's arm across her, listening and thinking how odd it was to have hail in August. Tony was face downwards, snoring gently into the pillow. With a clap of thunder, the hail turned to torrential rain and the bedroom was illuminated for a second as if by a firework. Anne had always found storms exciting. She began to stroke Tony's arm gently, feeling the hairs lifting in the air beneath her hand, shifting under its weight. The rain was sluicing down the walls; the road below the house was gurgling like a river. She lifted his heavy fingers and moved them on to her breast and felt them stir and tighten as he turned sleepily towards her, all soft and blurred against her electric, tingling body until a second thunderburst woke him entirely.

Anne was half-woken again an hour or so later by the slamming of car doors and Rod and Nancy running up their path, one of them dropping a bunch of keys, scuffles and squeals of laughter and the front door crashing shut. It was still bucketing down outside. She heard Rod and Nancy's feet on their stairs; they seemed to be chasing each other from room to room. She thought of hamsters racing round a cage, snuggled into Tony and went back to sleep. Only to be drilled awake again by what she thought was the alarm clock and turned into a persistent ringing of the front door bell.

Tony struggled into his pajama trousers, Anne into her nightdress, clumsy with sleep and terror that something had happened to one of the children. Nancy and Rod, hair plastered down by the rain, stood dripping on the doorstep.

"We've been burgled," said Rod.

"No! Have you called the police?" Tony was rubbing his eyes blearily.

"Of course I have! They're on their way. The thing is, did you see or hear anything?"

"No, not a sound."

"Nothing at all.. Or we'd have been round there, wouldn't we, Tony?"

"Rod's workroom's been completely ransacked. They've taken his Compaq, everything. They even took the Thomas the Tank Engine mouse mat that I gave him for his birthday. And the rain's pouring through the bedroom ceiling," Nancy wailed.

"Oh, you poor things! And you're shivering. Come in, I'll get you a hot drink."

"Can I have hot chocolate?" hiccupped Nancy as they trekked mud into the front room. The Lees could smell alcohol gusting out of them.

"'Course you can, love. If we've got any. Rod?"

"Decaf. Black, one sugar. Look this isn't a social call, you know. Are you sure you didn't hear anything? Or notice anybody suspicious hanging round earlier? Any of the local oiks? Leave the front door, Tony, we want to hear the police."

"Oh we'll hear them, don't worry. Good night out, was it?"

Tony draped a jacket round Nancy's shoulders and guided her to a chair.

"What? Of course, they've all got serial numbers, everything's registered. Should be easy enough for the police to trace, I suppose."

Tony was shaking his head doubtfully. "I take it you were insured?"

"Don't be stupid, that's not the point. What I am supposed to do in the meantime? Start again from scratch? I've lost irreplaceable data as well." Rod slumped on to the sofa and dropped his head into his hands. "I'm really up shit creek now."

Tony was reminded of a broken toy robot with all the colored wires hanging out.

"They're here!" Nancy jumped up at the sound of a siren and sank again when Tony said, "That's a fire engine. There'll be a lot of flooding tonight."

"Oh my God, the roof! Have you got a tarpaulin or something?"

Anne came in with a tray and two towels. She threw one to Rod.

"Why did everything have to happen at once?" Nancy sobbed. "Why did we have to get burgled and the roof leak on the same night. It isn't fair! And I've got to be at the bloody airport at dawn."

"It never rains but it pours," said Tony.

"Is that supposed to be funny? Because it's in pretty poor taste if it is. If you two had been a bit more vigilant, a bit more neighborly, instead of snoring away while some villain was breaking into our house—" Rod half-rose from the sofa.

"Drink your coffee," said Tony. "I might be able to get you a bit of tarp in the morning."

"Your poor little dress!" Anne sympathized. It had shriveled like an old-fashioned bathing suit. "And Rod, your trousers have really shrunk too."

"They're not my trousers," said Rod. "Or my Y-fronts."

"Whatever turns you on," said Tony.

"Could you *make* a tarpaulin, Tony? Out of some black sacks or something?" asked Nancy. "Anne, please don't rub my hair like that. You should *blot* hair, never rub it. You've got things like buckets and washing up bowls, haven't you? Could we borrow them, only we've put down our dinner service and mugs and stuff to catch the drips but they're not very deep."

"Sounds as if you've got a tile or two missing," said Tony. "I can hear a car. I think that's them now."

"You took your time! No wonder the crime rate's so bloody high," Anne and Tony heard Rod greet the police.

"You didn't have your woowoos on," Nancy was complaining. "I wanted to hear your woowoos."

Anne said, "I'm ashamed of you, Tony Lee, being so unneighborly. The least you could've done was to get up your ladder in the dark and the rain and make a tarpaulin out of black sacks."

"You might have been a bit more vigilant yourself. Rubbing that poor girl's hair like that. It'll be interesting to see if we get our towels back. Let's try to get some sleep for what's left of the night, or is it dawn already?"

Lying in bed again, they heard the police leaving. The rain had slackened and the voices carried clearly.

"That's your car, is it, sir, the one parked over the curb? You did say you drove home, didn't you?"

"Oh no. I know your game. You're not going to get me on that one. The neighbors gave us a drink, you can ask them."

"We will, sir. Somebody will probably be round to talk to them tomorrow."

"Just who's supposed to be the criminal here anyway?"

"Will someone be coming to counsel us, from Victim Support or something?" said Nancy.

"I'll have a word if you like, madam."

"OK, only could they ring first because I've got a really heavy week."

"Oh Rodney, Rodney," said Tony, wiping tears of laughter with the corner of his pillow. "Still, he's right. They can't touch him for the drink driving. But he won't be seeing those state-of-the-art computers again."

"It was only this morning that it really hit me, Lyris," Anne said. "You know, the thought of somebody breaking in while we were asleep a few feet away. It's horrible to know somebody was going through all their things, touching personal things, things of sentimental value. They say you feel violated. I do, and it wasn't even me. I felt quite sick. You have to feel sorry for them in spite of everything."

"I suppose so. There's some tea with ginger somewhere if you're still feeling sick." Lyris spoke listlessly. She was still in John's dressing gown at midday and she hadn't done her hair. The telephone rang and she made no move to answer.

"Do you want me to get it?"

"No, let it ring, thank you. Oh, all right. If it's that nuisance Zoe, I've gone away and you don't know when I'll be back."

"By the way—" Anne started to say but decided against speaking too soon.

"It was Zoe," she said when she returned. "I told her you'd gone to visit your brother in New Zealand. She seemed very put out."

"Excellent. Thank you. That should have got rid of her for once and for all. Perhaps everybody will leave me in peace now."

"Talking of feeling sick, do you know what Tony said to me this morning?"

Lyris just sat there like Old Nokomis with a pigtail down her back.

"He said that Rod and Nancy would have to change their lifestyle when the baby arrives. Well, I don't think even she suspects anything yet, but he's never wrong about that."

"Well, I wish he'd come and read my tea leaves or look into his crystal ball for me—but perhaps I'm better off not knowing."

She wished Anne would go. The last thing she was interested in was Miss Nancy's possible confinement. In truth, she wasn't interested in anything.

Anne sighed, racking her brains for something to talk about but not wanting to go rattling on. Her account of last night's adventure hadn't raised a smile, not even the woowoos or Rod and Nancy's dinner service set out on the bedroom floor or Nancy asking Tom to make a tarpaulin, like Katharine Hepburn asking Humphrey Bogart to make a torpedo in *The African Queen*. It wasn't every night that the house next door was burgled while you were asleep, specially when you might not have been asleep at all, but she couldn't say that to Lyris. Should she offer something about her children or the garden, Di and Dodi, Tony Blair?

"Looks like we're in for some more rain," she said. "Would you like me to run the Hoover over the front hall and the stairs? No?"

Not that she wanted to, but the house had a worrying air of neglect. She would rather have been reading in the garden or just dozing in the sun.

"Did I tell you that my niece had her baby, a little girl? They've called her Paige."

"Page? It sounds like—something out of a book."

"It does rather. How's that great nephew of yours these days? Has he been getting himself in the papers again recently?"

"Please never mention his name in this house again."

It occurred to Anne that Lyris, who had seemed to be coping so well, had been struck by belated mourning. It was all too easy to assume that people got over bereavements; in the old days they could wear a black diamond on their sleeves or a black armband to remind you, but you never saw that now.

"I really miss John, you know," she said.

"So do I, my dear. So do I."

CHAPTER EIGHTEEN

Nathan, whose name was never to be spoken again, had made her laugh with his description of Soho, but Lyris found herself thinking back to happier times spent there. He thought he was so trendy with his talk of the pink pound, but he'd never drunk in the Fitzroy Tavern in its heyday. Nor had she really, because women weren't exactly welcomed with open arms, but it had its place in her mental map of the area. Fitzrovia. She had heard that it was fashionable again. Her great friend Molly Levinson had had a flat in Percy Street. They had met when Lyris designed the costumes for a production of the Čapeks' *Insect Play* at the Unity Theatre. Molly had painted the scenery. Funny, generous Molly was the last person you would have suspected of having up her sleeve the mean trick of dying at fifty-five. Bangles and bracelets rattled on the arm she tucked into Lyris's as the two of them wandered mazily through Soho streets in a long noon that stretched into evening, deep in conversation, laughing.

Molly could cook for thirty or more people in her tiny kitchen, and somehow make it elegant, with everybody crammed into her sitting room and bedroom, plates, glasses, ashtrays on her dressing-table. There was hardly space for more than the easel in her studio. She had a mass of loose blonde curls and dark sherry-colored eyes, a tragic profile and a full mouth that looked hurt but opened in a wide smile to light up her whole face. She loved to dance, on her long straight legs that tapered to small feet; she loved shoes. If Molly hadn't upped and died on her, perhaps they might have made a home together now. Lyris couldn't remember a single quarrel or serious disagreement except about the men that Molly got involved with. Molly never had any luck with men, falling in love with a succession of rotters. She could spot a wrong 'un from the top of a bus, John used to say, and would jump off to invite him to dinner. The unspeakable youth had remarked on Molly's portrait in the bedroom. "That is my best friend, Molly Levinson," she'd said.

And now she was sitting at the kitchen table, the archetypal woman in a dressing gown. Old woman in a dressing gown. No need to get dressed now, it would soon be late enough to go to bed. No need to water the garden. Anne had been right; vertical rain was splashing down as if poured through an enormous colander. Let the fruit rot on the vines; the snails were welcome to it.

Beyond belief, someone was ringing at the door. Rattling the letterbox, calling into the hall, "Please let me in."

It wouldn't go away.

"Please open the door."

Lyris went through at last, shuffling over the free newspapers that lay there, and put the chain on the door. She could see a mouth through the letterbox, wet lips and teeth. She opened the door a crack and saw a young woman, soaked to the skin. She removed the chain and opened the door.

"What do you want? What do you mean by battering on my door and shouting like that? Are you selling dusters or ironing-board covers? If so you've picked the wrong day, and the wrong house."

"No. It's me!"

"Who are you? Am I supposed to know you?"

"It's Jacki. I came to the funeral with Nathan."

"Nathan! Did he send you? If so, you can clear off. I don't care how wet you are."

"No, he didn't, I promise. I haven't seen him. Please let me in, I can explain." She was holding an umbrella blown inside out and broken.

"It had better be a very good explanation."

Lyris stood back to let Jacki in.

"Come through to the kitchen. Mind those pictures with your wet sleeve! Are you sure you're Jacki? You look different."

"I am different. I've changed. You'll see. I've even changed the way I spell my name."

But why should I want to see? What is it to me? Lyris thought. Jacki's shoes sloshed with every step.

"For goodness sake peel that raincoat off. You can stay till you're a bit drier, then you'll have to leave. I was about to have a bath and an early night. Empty your shoes in the sink. Here, catch." Lyris tossed her the kitchen towel and Jacki tipped out her shoes and began to rub her hair.

Lyris watched her as she toweled away, wringing out her hair and wiping her face.

"I know what's different about you. Weren't you black the last time I saw you?"

Jacki started to cry.

"Oh my dear. I'm so sorry. How tactless of me. I suppose you must have that skin condition that poor Michael Jackson suffers from. But you shouldn't be embarrassed, it really quite suits you to be white."

It was fascinating, putting Jacki in an altogether more interesting light, but she went on crying.

"I can see that it might cause problems for you, but you must accept that pigment is not immutable. Think of those paintings where the yellow has vanished, making green leaves blue."

"It isn't that. I never was black, I only wanted to be. I'm crying because it's all been so horrible and you're being so kind."

"Kind? Me? What nonsense. You've just got thoroughly

chilled and now you're in the warm and it's making you emotional. You'd better take those wet things off, I suppose. Come upstairs with me and I'll lend you something to go home in."

Jacki thought it would be better to wait until she was wearing Mrs. Crane's clothes before telling her that she had no home to go to. Her own bags, which were saturated anyway, and the bin liners could wait where she'd left them at the side of the porch till later.

"Haven't you got a lot of books?" she said. "I used to work in a library. Some of them look really old. Are they first editions?"

"Probably. Covered in mildew and dust, I'm ashamed to admit. Haven't been opened for years. Come along, let's find something to fit you. I must say your hair is an improvement."

"I nearly scalped myself cutting it off."

As Lyris pulled from a cupboard the bag of garments she'd been meaning to take to the Geranium Shop for the Blind, a revelation punched her in the stomach. Jacki was pregnant. An embryonic Nathan was curled up asleep under the sodden cardigan. Why else would Jacki have appeared on her doorstep like an orphan of the storm? She scrabbled out a pair of trousers, a shirt and a ball of socks.

"You say you haven't seen Nathan?"

"No. He doesn't want to know. He's completely blanked me."

"What about his parents then? Have you been to see them?"

"Them! They threw me out in the street."

Jacki's teeth were chattering and her arms—she had taken off her cardigan—were goosepimpled and blue.

"Your own parents then? I assume you have some?"

"I didn't like to bother them with it."

So that leaves me, thought Lyris. And a rough beast slouching to Dulwich to be born.

"The bathroom's through there. Have a hot shower if you want. I'll be in the kitchen. I suppose you're hungry."

"Mrs. Crane?"

Lyris turned at the head of the stairs.

"You're an angel!"

And if you think I'm going to be left holding the baby, you've got another think coming, madam.

An hour later Jacki had her feet, in a pair of thick woollen socks, under the kitchen table; she was almost too cozy now because warm air had swept in as the rain stopped and the kitchen was steamed up from the boiling of potatoes and runner beans, but she wriggled her toes blissfully as she ate. There was a bottle of wine on the table. Jacki was laughing. Lyris was laughing. So great was Lyris's relief when they had cleared up their misunderstanding that she had insisted that Jacki stay the night.

"So you see, Mrs. Crane, really Marsha did me a favor. She made me take a long hard look at myself and my life. OK, so I'm out of a job as a result of not going back into work, but it's been a valuable period of personal growth for me. A learning curve. I changed my name back to Jacki and I realized that if I couldn't be like Marsha at least I could learn to like myself."

"Can a leopard change its spots . . .?" murmured Lyris.

"I'm doing something about those as well. My complexion's got a lot better since I haven't been so stressed out."

"Or an Ethiopian his skin, I was going to add. Or, in your case, an Englishwoman."

"Anyway, I decided to try to do good in small ways, like taking my bottles back to the Body Shop for recycling."

"Your friend Marsha sounds eminently sensible. I think she's right—you should drop that tribunal for unfair dismissal. I don't think you've got a very strong case."

"Oh God, my bags! They're still out there on the step. I'll just go and get them in. There's something else I've got to tell you in a minute."

CHAPTER NINETEEN

He had sent flowers to Jenny as a matter of course but Clovis was under no illusion that they would erase the memory of his awful behavior. He was sitting in the back of the shop, a boor with a sore head growling over the top of *The Bookseller* at anybody who had the temerity to speak to him. He had woken to the realization that not only had he been unforgivably rude to Nancy but she would be descending the following day with a belligerent author from Singapore who expected to find an audience. How could he possibly conceal the event from Candy and prevent her from turning up like the trouper she was? If she were to meet Nancy and think that he had been fraternizing behind her back it would seem the most appalling insult. It would finish her off. His mouth and nose were full of the fumes of a smelly cheese Jenny and Christopher had brought back from France and a postcard from Miranda did nothing to take away the taste of rottenness. He had forgotten she was on holiday. He was a failure as a father. Examination of a plastic bag in the bathroom had revealed a pair of soaking chinos and underpants with a purplish stain.

Unable to face them and not wanting Mrs. Evans who came in to clean once a week to find them, he had pushed the bag to the back of the wardrobe.

★   ★   ★

"What's up with you, darling? Hangover?" asked Candy when she dropped in to find him morosely contemplating his inadequacies as a parent, husband, friend and bookseller.

"You could say that."

"Stay there, I'll fix you my patent remedy. 'Tis efficacious in every case."

"No, I don't want it. You really must curb your Sally Bowles tendencies, you know. I shouldn't have said that, I'm sorry. Look, Candy, could you hold the fort for a few minutes while I look for a catalogue in the shed?"

He sat on a bundle of nibbled newspapers watching a wood-louse. He shouldn't have said it. He should have swallowed his medicine; Candy's Prairie Oyster was as much as he deserved. He imagined Mrs. Evans going through his wardrobe and finding Rod's things. Whatever would she think? He usually avoided her because she was Welsh and knew that Clovis was the Welsh version of Lewis. Now he could never face her again. In fact, his mother had taken his name from the stories of Saki, and clove carnations were her favorite flowers. She had had money of her own and it was this that made it possible for him to keep Criterion Books afloat. Then, like a wet smack in the face, he remembered that he had promised to return Rod's clothes to Nancy at the reading.

Candy was putting Queen Victoria's *Letters* into a bag when he went back.

"Enjoy," she said to a customer, smiling. Then turned a hurt face on Clovis when they were alone.

"I'll be going then, if I've fulfilled my usefulness. I've got to go to the Edgware Road."

"Not 'A Little Place off the Edgware Road', I trust?"

"No. Sorry to disappoint you. Actually, it's quite big."

"Look Candy, I really am sorry. I don't know what's the matter with me lately."

"Guilty conscience perhaps, darling?"

"What makes you say that?"

"Nothing in particular. Just that often when people are angry with themselves they take it out on those closest to them. By the way, in case you're interested, Sherpa's had his shot and he's feeling better already."

Apart from everything else, Candy thought as she waited for a bus, it wasn't fair that Clovis could have a hangover and just look a bit tired around the eyes, which only added to his world-weary charm. He had hurt her very deeply with that Sally Bowles crack, throwing her past in her face. If he was to turn nasty on her, who would she have? Billy and five dogs she'd never wanted in the first place. Where had all her girlfriends gone? Some were married, some were dead. She hadn't enjoyed Barb and Sam's barbecue; they were very nice but she hadn't really fitted in. Everybody else was in couples and she'd been years older than all of them. Besides Clovis was no angel himself. He and Izzie might try to pass off their marriage as a casualty of the town mouse/country mouse syndrome, but Clovis had admitted to her that he had several affairs before the divorce.

Clovis recognized that his poisonous frame of mind dated from his journey home from the private view. As he could do nothing to make amends there, he'd better try to be a bit more dutiful elsewhere. He rang Lyris, only to get some girl who said that Mrs. Crane was in a meeting, and could she take a message. Extraordinary. How could Lyris possibly be in a meeting?

"Just tell her that I'll pick her up on my way to Isobel's if she wants a lift. I'm hiring a car. There'll be two of us, tell her. It's Clovis Ingram."

"No problem, Mr. Ingram."

If only, thought Clovis. Next he tried Nancy Carmody, to cancel the reading, but got her voice mail which told him that she would be out of the office all day. Like a fool he put down the phone without leaving a message, to see Sidney Leeds bustling through the door, followed by Lucinda.

"Good morrow, good morrow! And how wags the world with you this merry morn? Strike while the iron's hot, eh? I thought you'd want to get cracking on the details of my reading, so I've drawn up a list of the people you should invite. Lucinda, light of my life, give the gentleman the guest list."

An hour or so later he tried Nancy again and left a message asking her to call him the next morning. It occurred to him that the cancellation would place him even lower in Jenny and Christopher's estimation. And there was the matter of Rod's wet washing. He rang Candy early in the evening.

"How was the Edgware Road?"

"Fine."

"Good. Get what you wanted?"

"Yes thanks."

"Is this a bad time? Are you busy?"

"Yes it is. And I am rather."

He could hear canned laughter in the background.

"I won't keep you then. I was just wondering what you were doing tomorrow?"

There was a hurt pause. This is just like a conversation with Isobel, he thought. Then Candy said, "It's my mother's birthday. I'm taking her some flowers. Why? What's that? Did you just say, 'There *is* a God'? You did, under your breath. I heard you."

He had forgotten that it was the date of Candy's annual

pilgrimage to her mother's grave with a replica of her carnival queen's bouquet.

"No. I mean yes—at times like these, sad anniversaries and so forth, we find our thoughts turning on—find ourselves examining our beliefs, clinging on to a hope that there is some kind of afterlife . . ."

"Well, yes. But I never knew you did. Anyway, I'm going to Cambury. Did you want me in the shop?"

"Absolutely not. You go off and enjoy yourself—I mean, when do you think you'll be back? You could look up some old friends, make a night of it—stay over."

"I haven't got any old friends. Have you gone mad, Clovis, or are you drunk?"

"No, it just seems a bit of a waste to go all that way just to come straight back."

"Well it might to you. I won't get back till around nine anyway."

You take your time, Clovis thought.

"I'll be thinking of you then. Take care of yourself," he said.

"OK. You too. Bye."

As he was telling Candy to take care of herself, he suddenly saw her in a low-cut swimming costume, with a round pink scar on the suntanned skin of her back. He hadn't liked to say anything but it looked as if it might have been made by the tip of a cigar.

Meanwhile, Nathan was mooching along the Mile End Road. The East End was the territory allocated to him by Josh's mother who had issued each of Josh's friends with a photograph and ordered them to take to the streets. She had stuck up pictures of Josh in shops and supermarkets, the Group's local, the White Bear, and in the French Pub, the Colony Room and the Fridge in Brixton. She seemed to have totally lost it, accosting people in the street and haranguing bouncers outside clubs, and she'd been escorted out of the Atlantic Bar and Grill and told not to come back. Seb had seen her pulling homeless people out of their sleeping-bags in the Strand. Nathan had been to Hoxton Square where he'd had a drink with some people he knew and checked out a couple of new galleries and the Whitechapel and Flowers East and called in at a letting agency, which was a bit of a joke really in the circumstances. So even though the day hadn't been entirely wasted, he still felt so depressed he didn't know what to do with himself.

He went into a gloomy tavern where a handful of terminally sad old gits were scattered around not watching the American football on the big screen, and took his beer to a corner table. He tried to analyze his state of mind. If he was honest he wasn't that affected by Josh's disappearance, even when he'd imagined himself identifying the body in some mortuary. It had occurred to him that Josh's mother might be willing to let him make a death-mask. Works by his contemporaries, composed of blood and bodily fluids, passed through his brain. You poor sick sod, he thought, that's your friend you've got spread out on the dissecting table. He took the photo of Josh from his pocket and stared at it. Josh, blond, green-eyed, suited up for a family wedding, looked like a different person from the one he knew.

He remembered fantasizing about snuff videos, and the notion of his *Diary of a Young Artist*. He hadn't even made a start on that. He was mentally exhausted. All the inspiration had gone out of him. Maybe all artists had to go through this, but at the moment all his ideas seemed crap. He was totally empty. Perhaps he should forget about the computer and move on to Minimalism. It seemed to be the way things were going. Lyris's words about paint came back to him and the memory of lying in her garden. It was her fault he was so depressed. He wouldn't be surprised if he was on the verge of a breakdown. Going round the galleries in the afternoon hadn't helped and he'd had to face the truth about where he had gone wrong as an artist. He had been arrogant and shortsighted. He had been left way behind; the people who were enjoying most fame and success were those who had had the sense to get themselves a publicist before they even had a gallery.

When he had rung Louis Viner some woman had said that Louis was in Italy. So much for the studio visit then, he supposed that was way down on Louis's list of priorities. He'd forgotten to ask how John's show was going. He still hadn't done anything about that purse, apart from borrow the money in it. He was boracic, thanks to being so liberal with the last of the money Dad had sent him, and he could use that twenty now that he'd given to baby Jack. He'd been counting on Dad slipping him a bit, but somehow it got overlooked this time. He supposed he'd have to sign on again if he could. Zoe was coming tomorrow to look at his work, but the way he was feeling, he couldn't give a toss. He felt like the deflated blow-up of Munch's screamer in his room. Somebody had pulled the plug on him.

CHAPTER TWENTY

The smell of coffee drifted into the bedroom as Lyris, in pleasurable half-sleep, anticipated John's step on the stair.

"Good morning! I couldn't remember how you like it so I've put milk and sugar on the tray."

Jacki was putting a tray on the bedside table, pulling back the curtain to let a shaft of sunshine in. Lyris had been so aware of the empty space beside her in the bed, so comfortable dozing in an ordinary morning, that she had been sure she would open her eyes to see John there in his dressing gown. Desolation swept over her. Jacki was standing smiling, in Lyris's clothes.

"Close the curtain please, the sun's hurting my eyes."

"Sorry. I've brought a cup for myself, hope you don't mind."

Lyris sat up.

"Jacki, if you're going to stay on here, there are a few things we'd better get clear."

"Absolutely. I'm all for ground rules. I wouldn't dream of invading your personal space, Mrs. Crane." Jacki poured herself a cup of coffee and sat down on the edge of the bed.

Lyris had had a bad night, waking at four from a dream of Nathan bringing back her purse to feelings of rage and humiliation exacerbated by the hour, and by the knowledge that Jacki was in her house. Although Jacki had been vehement in her condemnations of

Nathan, Lyris could not bring herself to tell her that he had stolen from her. It had taken her a long time to get back to sleep.

"But why me?" she had asked the night before.

She knew that it was bad form for an old person to suggest that a young one was a social failure, one had to pretend that they all led exciting and dissolute lives, but really, had the girl no friends at all of her own age? She had expressed appropriate horror when Jacki explained that the house she lived in had been turned into a crack den and how the Yardie's bullet, missing her by inches, had been the final straw.

"I've never forgotten your face at your husband's funeral, how it looked really kind and sympathetic. We didn't really get the chance to talk, understandably, but I knew instinctively you would be somebody I could relate to on a deeper level."

"But Jacki, I'm not a nice person at all. I'm not kind. I'm a selfish, grumpy old artist who has got used to living alone and thinking about nothing but my work."

"I might be able to help you there," Jacki had said.

They drank their coffee thinking their own thoughts until Jacki broke the silence.

"Bathroom's free by the way. I had my bath earlier. Let me know when you're ready for me to make a start on cataloguing those drawings. Or I could get on with the books, it's up to you."

By mid-morning Lyris had retreated into the garden with a pad of paper. Jacki's damp duvet, retrieved from its bin liner, slumped over the washing line and assorted garments were steaming gently. Trapped in their shadows, Lyris had no option but to take her pencil and begin drawing Jacki's clothes. Inside, Jacki was happy. She had come to believe her own story and forget that she had fled her flat because she simply couldn't bear to spend another night alone, and she had telephoned her mother to explain about her new job and change of address. "Dulwich, that sounds like a step up," Mum had said with cautious optimism. Jacki, looking out on the quiet street, saw a washing-machine repair van pulling up outside. A man got out and took a heavy-looking box from the back seat.

Lyris heard Jacki calling, "Mrs. Crane, it's Tony for you."

As the morning passed and Nancy was apparently still out of the office and hadn't returned his first call, Clovis became reconciled to the reading. Candy and the dogs were doubtless safely on the Cambury train. The trouble was, without Candy, who would be his audience? He could hardly expect Jenny and Christopher to hike out from Highgate. He considered ringing up a few people and calling in some favors, but as he had no idea of the writer's name he felt that he might look rather foolish. Billy was the other regular and he could be introduced as a fellow writer. He could be relied on to ask a question in the awkward silence that usually followed the reading. Clovis stuck the Back in Five Minutes notice on the door and went to Criterion Cleaners to place his fate in Billy and Belinda's hands.

"Can you do these for this afternoon?" he asked.

"Going somewhere special?" said Belinda holding up the stained Calvins.

"They're not mine. And look, there's a perfectly rational explanation but I'd rather you didn't say anything to Candy. Where's Billy?"

"Over there, sitting at the sewing machine. Under the sign that says Invisible Menders."

Billy came through and took over.

"Yes, we can have these as good as new for you by five o'clock. No problem."

"That's great. Thanks, Billy. By the way, I've got a last-minute reading at the shop tonight. Author from Singapore. I feel very privileged to get him—he's not very well-known here yet but he's massive on the Malay Peninsula. Seven o'clock. Bring a few friends along if you like."

"Sounds like my kind of guy," said Belinda.

"That desperate is it, Clovis?" Billy asked.

"I'm afraid so. Look, I'd be very grateful if you could drum up a few people. There'll be some wine. And both of you, I do think it would be better if you didn't mention anything at all about it to Candy. I'd hate her to feel left out."

Belinda and Billy were looking at him curiously.

"Tell you what, Billy, why don't you just drop the cleaning off when you come later? I'd better go or there'll be queues all round the block."

With that sorted, Clovis put up a board outside the shop announcing Author Reading and Signing. Tonight at 7 P.M., with very little expectation that it would bring in any punters.

By seven forty-five the audience, Billy, Lee Kwan Kwok from the Wayang restaurant, Barb and Sam, was growing restless. There was no eminent author, no Nancy and there were no crisps left. Barb remarked that they were surprised that Candy wasn't there. Clovis could see that Billy was furious that his triumph in capturing Lee was turning to embarrassment, and he himself was suffering severe loss of face.

"This sucks," said Sam. "I'm starving." She turned to Lee. "Why don't we all go round to your restaurant?"

The audience exited *en masse*. Damn Nancy. Like father, like daughter. The no-show Carmodys. For this he had compromised himself with Billy and Belinda who no doubt imagined some guest of his had fled half-naked into the night, he had disappointed Lee Kwan Kwok and probably blackballed himself at a very convenient restaurant. He had also failed to anticipate the Sam and Barb danger and was sure it was only a matter of time before they blabbed to Candy. He finished off the third bottle of wine which he had opened in desperation as conversation petered out, and considered parceling up Rod's clothes and addressing then to Rayner's wife in the hope that they would cause a few unpleasant moments in the Carmody household. Before locking up, he hurled the Criterion Cleaners bag out of the back door. The foxes could have it.

CHAPTER TWENTY-ONE

"Nathan, telephone for you! Nathan! Phone!"

The hammering in Nathan's dream became somebody banging on his door. He stumbled across the room, bashing his shins on one of the large cartons on the floor. Ramesh from the ground floor was standing there.

"You're wanted on the phone."

"Right."

Nathan pushed past him, ran downstairs and picked up the phone.

"By the way Nathan, I'm moving out today."

"Yeah, right. Tara then. Hello? Nathan speaking."

"This is Joshua's mother. Tell your friends they can call off the search."

Josh was dead. He couldn't believe it. After saying it, she'd just put the phone down. He wanted to call her back and ask if she was sure. It had to be a mistake, Josh couldn't be dead. But she sounded like she was crying and her hysterical voice had left him in no doubt. And calling him Joshua. He dialed Howard's number.

"Howard? It's Nathan. Yeah, all right. You? Listen Howard, Josh's mother just called me and apparently Josh is, Josh is, well apparently he's—dead."

"Dead? He can't be! Why? How?"

"I don't know, do I? She just called me. Look, Howard, I can't handle this. Can you let the others know? I'll catch up with you later."

He walked back to his room in a daze. What the fuck was he supposed to do now? What did you do with yourself when somebody you knew just died? He knelt on the floor and pulled open the flaps of one of the boxes that had been waiting in the hall when he got back the day before. Karla, who had the room next to Nathan's, told him they had been delivered by a bloke driving a florist's van. "Tell Nathan Buster sent them," was all he'd said.

Nathan ripped his knuckle on a rusty staple. His fantasy about Josh on a mortuary slab and a dissecting table came back in a guilty rush; supposing Josh had already been dead then and could tune into people's minds and know what they were thinking? He sucked his knuckle, tasting rusty blood. How could he even have contemplated a death-mask, plastering clay over Josh's face, feeling the eyeballs under his closed lids, sealing his nose, making a mould as if Josh himself was only a piece of sculpture with no feelings? He must have been insane. Nobody warned you what it was really like, somebody's mother crying over the phone, everything out of focus, this feeling as if everything was draining away around you and from you, and all the memories starting to flood in.

Earlier, before Nathan had heard the news, Zoe was angry if not altogether surprised not to find him at his studio at the appointed time. Seb was there working, while someone called Mitchell was hanging around drinking coffee. There was a faint smell of rotten meat and old ganja in the air. Zoe felt oppressed by the building, but she could see that its burned-out dereliction would contrast well with Lyris's sub-urban street. She knew the old cow hadn't really gone to New Zealand but was just being contrary. She was probably in a flap because she hadn't bothered to send in her CV.

"So where is he then?" Zoe demanded.

"I would have thought you'd be the one to know that," said Seb.

She could see him trying to look down the front of her dress.

"Why? He was supposed to meet me here at ten so that I can look at his work."

"Typical Nathan," said Mitchell.

"I can show you round if you like. Not that there's much to see," Seb offered.

"I really need Nathan to talk me through it."

She took out her mobile. Mitchell and Seb watched as she flicked through her diary to find Nathan's number.

"Engaged."

"Do you want a coffee or a Coke or something?"

"No thanks. This is ridiculous, it's ringing now but nobody's answering."

"He's probably still in bed, knowing him. Dead to the world. Why don't you go and see?"

"I haven't got his home address. Is it far?"

"You mean you haven't been there? It's only round the corner."

As Zoe went down the stairs Seb said, "I thought it was too good to be true as soon as she walked in, Nathan with Zoe. He was batting way out of his league."

The only reason Zoe had agreed to have a drink with Nathan after that private view was to pick his brains about Lyris, but both Lyris and Nathan were proving to be such pains that Zoe was tempted to walk away from the whole project. However, she had pushed the film so hard that she wasn't going to risk losing her credibility by backing out now. The front door stood open and Zoe met an Indian bloke carrying his bags out to a taxi.

"I'm looking for Nathan."

"You're welcome to him. First floor, on the right."

When she'd gone upstairs she pushed the door, which was slightly ajar, and stopped on the threshold. Nathan was sitting on the floor in tears wearing only a pair of crumpled boxers, surrounded by cartons and electronic equipment and cables. He slammed his fist down on a Compaq computer as she came into the room.

"Nathan! What on earth's the matter?"

"This bastard anorak thing! It's got all bits and pieces of different hardware and modems and systems, and I haven't got a clue how to set the bastard up."

"I could probably sort it out for you if I had time. There's no need to cry over a pc."

"It's not just the computer." Nathan snorted and wiped his hand across his nose. "I've just heard that a friend of mine is dead. He was only my age."

"Oh God, I'm really sorry, Nathan. I don't know what to say. How did he like die, did he have AIDS or was he on something? It wasn't suicide, was it? You're not telling me he was *murdered*? Or was it in a car crash?"

"Will you just shut the fuck up? How the bloody hell do I know? I only just heard. His mother rang me. He probably was using. He was into all sorts lately. All I know is, he's dead. My mate Josh is dead."

"Well, excuse me for trying to show a bit of sympathy. I would have thought the least you could have done was to *ask*. Look Nathan, I'm really sorry about your friend, but are we going to look at your work or not? I've already wasted like half the morning."

"Yeah, all right. What's the difference?"

As he pulled shorts and a T-shirt from the tangle of clothes on the unmade bed Zoe forced up the sash window and wondered what she was doing here in the armpit of Tufnell Park.

*　　*　　*

They were all there when Nathan and Zoe arrived, Seb, Mitch, Howard, Larry, all the Group except Josh, sitting around drinking vodka out of mugs.

"I just wish I could've told him, you know. I just wish I could've put my arm round him and given him a hug and said 'I love you, man'," Howard was saying while the others nodded. Seb buried his face in the crook of his arm, his body shaking. Mitchell blew his nose.

"Nathan! Tell us what happened! What did Josh's mother say?"

Confronted with the others' grief, Nathan felt new tears stinging his swollen face.

"I—well only that we should call off the search. I was hoping one of you lot would have rung her back by now."

Nathan took a swig from the vodka bottle. As nobody offered her any Zoe did the same, wiping it first on her skirt.

"We're all going to Josh's house a bit later," said Seb. "We're going to get some flowers. Are you two coming?"

"Not me," said Zoe. "I'm out of here. I mean, this is obviously a guy thing and I never even met him. I'll call you, Nathan."

She collided with two people in the doorway. Josh walked in leaning on a stick, holding hands with Sophie, the defector from the Group. A white surgical dressing was fixed with strips of plaster to the crown of this head.

"You bastard, you're not dead!" Howard burst into tears.

"Hello, boys," said Sophie. She was wearing a short yellow dress.

"Nathan, you are a complete and utter prat!" Seb jumped up and swung a punch which caught the side of Nathan's jaw. Nathan grabbed him and tried to pummel his head.

"Hey, hey, break it up you two! What kind of a welcome is

this? OK, OK, shut up everybody, give me a chance and I'll explain—"

"Did somebody beat you up?" asked Larry.

"Yeah, an escalator, apparently. I was on another planet. Twisted my ankle, but it could have been a lot worse." He grinned and tapped the dressing on his head. "That was my mother. She was so relieved so see me that she cracked me with the omelette pan. It's only superficial. She sent us round to apologize to you guys."

"So it's 'us' now, is it?" Howard spat the words, his face contorted with rage. "Have you any idea what you put us through, pretending to be dead when all the time you were shacked up with her? Well you can stick your apologies and your explanations. As far as I'm concerned it's over. The Group's finished."

He knocked the vodka bottle to the floor and rushed out. Seb followed him. Nathan picked up the leaking bottle. He held it out to Larry who shook his head.

"No thanks, I'd better be going. Got a lot to catch up on."

"Yeah, me too," said Mitchell. "See you around, Nathan."

Nathan could see them in the street below, walking away together. He banged on the window, waving the bottle, shouting, "See you around, wankers!" They looked up, shrugged, and walked on.

"Come on, Josh, there's no point in hanging around here." Sophie tucked her arm through his.

"Right. Take it easy, Nathan."

"Is that all you've got to say?" said Nathan. He could feel a lump swelling up on his jaw.

"Anybody would think I'd been on holiday in the South of France," said Josh. "I'm sorry if I've let everybody down by not being dead. I'll try harder next time—as it was I only nearly lost my foot and spent several nights sleeping in the park with total amnesia—sorry if it wasn't good enough for you. And for your information, I only met up with Sophie a couple of days ago when she found me wandering round Camden Lock."

"Who gives a toss? What I can't forgive is what you did to your own mother."

CHAPTER TWENTY-TWO

Jacki shrank several inches when she opened the door to Zoe. Tall people always had that effect on her. Her skirt draped dowdily at the sight of Zoe's long brown legs and elegant feet in sandals that were just a wisp of gold thong.

"Hi, you must be Zoe. I'm Jacki. Come in, Mrs. Crane's expecting you."

Lyris *was* expecting her. Zoe had phoned from her mobile ten minutes earlier. She was shown into the front room.

"Have a seat, Mrs. Crane won't be long. Can I get you a coffee, I mean a cup of coffee, or a cold drink while you wait?"

"Just a glass of still mineral water would be fine."

"No problem, Zoe. Bless you!" she said as Zoe sneezed twice. "There's a box of tissues on that table beside you."

Jacki went out, shutting the door behind her, leaving Zoe in a faded green velvet chair. She reached for the tissues, reminded of the counseling sessions she'd attended during a career crisis. Who on earth was the girl in the Birkenstocks, she wondered. She lit a cigarette and shuddered, suddenly caught in the gaze of a cat in a picture on the wall. She was certain she hadn't seen it when she was here before, and the paint of the fur that made her skin crawl looked wet, glistening in thick black and white swirls. She moved to the sofa but the green eyes with huge gold-ringed pupils followed her round the room wherever she sat.

Her own eyes started pricking and she felt the dreaded, familiar, swelling of the lids, the stinging in her nose and tightening of the throat. There was a real cat somewhere in the room. She wasn't so suggestible that a painting could have that effect on her allergies. She made for the door, her eyes streaming now, and screamed as something sinuous and furry rubbed her leg and darted out in front of her.

Lyris Crane was standing in the hall with the original of the painted cat in her arms. "Ah, Zoe. So sorry to have kept you waiting. I see you've already met Melody—Jacki's named her after a school chum, Melody Eatwell, because she's got such a good appetite. We call this old bruiser Mr. Mephistopheles, don't we, Jacki? Do you want a tissue? These summer colds are the end, aren't they?"

Zoe stepped back in fear as Lyris held the disgusting object out to her.

"Keep that thing away from me!"

"Here's your mineral water, Zoe."

"I've got to get out. Let me pass, please. I told you I was allergic. I can't breathe."

Lyris opened the front door and Zoe rushed out. Lyris shut the cat in the studio and she and Jacki followed Zoe into the front garden.

"Jacki's been helping me to compile my curriculum vitae for you. Are we going to start filming soon?"

Zoe could breathe more easily now. She took a sip of tap water. It was tepid and probably swarming with micro-organisms. She'd had it with Lyris Crane, and Nathan Pursey, too.

"About the film, Lyris. There's been a bit of a glitch, I'm afraid. The thing is, there are other people besides me working on the project and what's happened is we're oversubscribed at the moment.

You mustn't take it as a personal rejection because everybody was like really enthusiastic about your work . . ."

"Oh dear, I am disappointed. I was so looking forward to being a Neglected Woman Artist. Never mind, I suppose somebody might die and I'd be in with a chance again?"

"Could be. Anyway, would you mind passing it on to Nathan for me? Only I'm flying to Cairo in the morning to stay with my father, so he won't be able to contact me."

Back to square one, thought Zoe as she walked round the corner to the car where Dan was waiting. Now she'd have to start all over again with some other evil old witch. Imagine hoping somebody would die just so that you could be in a film.

"Some people would stoop to anything to get their faces on the telly," she told Dan as she fastened her seat belt.

When Jacki opened the front door again later in the afternoon to see Nathan's sister Rachel standing there her instinct was to slam it shut.

"Jackee! What are you doing here? It *is* you, isn't it?"

"Hello, Rachel, long time no see."

"I nearly didn't recognize you, you look really pretty! Oh, sorry, I didn't mean—"

"It's OK. Did you want to see Mrs. Crane? She's in her studio."

Lyris was doing a crossword. She was beginning to feel a bit more at ease with having somebody around and under less compulsion to appear busy all the time, but she wondered when to broach the subject of Jacki's departure.

"Rachel! What a lovely surprise!"

When Rachel followed them into the kitchen she half-expected to see John there.

"Something smells nice," she said.

"I'm doing my rice 'n' peas for later," Jacki told her, a little defensively. After all, she supposed she was still entitled to use her one Caribbean recipe.

"I don't remember you having cats," said Rachel, looking at the bowls on the floor.

"They're new. Well, second-hand really. I discussed having them with a friend but I'd forgotten all about it until they arrived."

"I know this is going to sound awful," said Rachel, "but I've talked it over with Lisa and Hayley and they think I'm doing the right thing. I've come to warn you about my dad."

Lyris went cold. "Warn me?"

"He's got designs on your house. He's been trying to say that you can't cope on your own so that he can get his hands on the property. You know, that you've fallen down on the maintenance and it's too big for you now. I'm really sorry, Lyris, his words not mine. Plus he's put Nathan up to getting hold of your art collection."

Lyris twisted her hands together. The Purseys would not make her cry. She felt the hard gold of her wedding ring.

"I don't believe it. How could anybody be so wicked?" Jacki was saying. She began to cry.

Lyris stood up and paced round the kitchen, slamming her fist into her palm.

"Oh has he? Oh has he indeed? We'll see about that. Designs on my house? Buster Pursey doesn't know the meaning of the word design! Just let him try! And Nathan with my pictures? That's a joke! Over my dead body! Or not, as they will find out."

"I really am sorry, Lyris. I didn't mean to upset you. Don't you think you ought to sit down?"

"Don't worry, I'm not about to have a heart attack. I can't thank you enough for coming to warn me. I shall be on my guard! Forewarned is forearmed. As a matter of fact, Rachel, Jacki and I were just discussing the matter of redecorating. Weren't we, Jacki?"

"Were we? Oh yes, of course we were. After all, four arms are better than two."

They were drinking Pimms in the garden after supper, Lyris in a wicker chair and Jacki sitting on the studio step. The cats were stalking insects in the grass.

"You know, Jacki, I *have* been thinking about my CV. I've had a very fortunate life, blessed by spending most of it with the man I loved, privileged to have been able to do the work I love, although it's absolute hell sometimes. Your best paintings are usually the ones you see in your mind's eye. We were often on our uppers but we managed to travel a bit, roughing it. We both did a lot of teaching to make ends meet. Not having children was our greatest sorrow, apart from the deaths of family and friends of course. You know the portrait of my friend Molly, don't you?"

"She looks lovely," said Jacki wistfully.

Lyris smelled mingled Arpège and cigarette smoke.

"I'm one of the last few people who remembers John as a young man now. Soon there'll be nobody. The keeper of the flame. Everybody hates artists' widows, did you know that? By the way, don't let me forget to ring the gallery tomorrow."

"I'll do it, I'm good at chasing people up."

"In one way I'm grateful that John died when he did because he was becoming rather confused. I don't mean he was totally gaga, but it hurt so much to see the puzzled look he had sometimes, like Don Quixote or the White Knight. The Lees were wonderful with him. Do you know the Thomas Hardy poem "Afterwards"? That was John, a 'man who used to notice such things'."

"We didn't do Hardy at school but I really loved the film of *Tess*."

"You are allowed to go on reading once you've left school you know, Jacki."

"I do. In fact I've still got some library books out. I'm going to return them when I've lost a bit more weight."

"That's the spirit. But noticing things has always been my job too. I lost any illusion that I would be a great artist long ago but I *was* given a gift and I've spent my life serving it. I was sent to a school for a while where I was very unhappy, but what I remember most vividly about it is a jug of scarlet rosehips against a green classroom wall that suddenly brought me consolation on a dark afternoon. My role is to record such things not only for their intrinsic beauty and for myself, but on behalf of people whose hearts are touched in precisely the same way. The natural world, the physical world, whether it is the blossom that brings us up with a jolt spring after spring, or the light on water, the fold of a field, the curve of a bird's wings in flight or Concorde or the ellipse of a bowl; the angle of that roof over there. I paint according to my own vision and style but I feel myself very much as being part of a tradition too. Walter de la Mare expresses what I'm trying to tell you;

> Since that all things thou wouldst praise
> Beauty took from those who loved them
> In other days."

Lyris felt suddenly awkward, remembering where rabbiting on to somebody of Jacki's age had got her the last time. Jacki refilled their glasses from the glass jug which was almost invisible now as the inky darkness saturated the pale night sky.

"Do you think you could teach me to draw? They do say everybody can be taught. Not to be a great artist of course, but just, you know, the basics."

"Everybody can be taught. With one exception."

"Nathan Pursey," said Jacki.

CHAPTER TWENTY-THREE

Lyris slept uncharacteristically late on the morning of Isobel's birthday, perhaps because the morning was overcast, or because of the Pimms she had drunk in the evening or because there was no smell of coffee to wake her. Jacki slept on while Lyris bathed and dressed. She was just ready when Clovis pulled up outside. She could see a glamorous blonde woman dressed in pink in the back, wearing a pink cartwheel hat and what appeared to be a fur stole, quite unsuitable for the day, but which proved to be several little dogs. An enormous gift-wrapped package was propped on the seat beside her, touching the roof of the car. Lyris stepped over the Sunday paper lying on the mat and closed the front door behind her.

"Sorry we're a bit late," Clovis apologized after introducing Candy to Lyris. "I overslept and one of the dogs was sick. What with one thing and another . . . it doesn't augur well for the day ahead."

"Oh stop being so gloomy, darling," said Candy. "Still, I hope it does brighten up for Isobel. There's a really depressing feel to the day for some reason. I hope you don't mind having the windows open for the dogs," she added to Lyris.

"That's extraordinary," said Lyris as they passed a flower stall. "I'm sure that was Sonia Pursey, Nathan's mother, serving on that stall, and look at all the people round it. I thought Sonia had given up working on the stalls years ago. It can't be something like Mothering Sunday can it?"

She turned her head to look back. A beer barrel-bellied man in a vest was unloading flowers from the back of a van. She glimpsed his face with its mouthful of beaver-like teeth. "Yes, that's definitely one of the Floral King's stalls."

"Good thing I bought mine yesterday then," said Clovis. An enormous bunch of *mimosa pudica*, the sensitive plant, Izzie's favorite, spiked with roses, lay in the boot.

"Mind if we play some tapes?" Candy asked Lyris. "Or would you rather have the radio on?"

"No, not at all. Let's have some music."

Clovis pushed the button and Bette Midler flooded the car with "The Wind Beneath My Wings." Candy sang along with it.

Lyris closed her eyes, wondering whether she could ask Clovis to turn it down and wishing she hadn't seen Sonia. She still cherished a ridiculous hope that her purse would arrive in the post to show that Nathan had had a change of heart and was not entirely under Buster's thumb, but as the distance from home increased, her shame at the memory of her pitiful fantasies of friendship with Nathan receded. Naturally she had not passed on Zoe's message to him. In any case, she knew Zoe was as likely to be in Egypt as she herself was to be in New Zealand. She dozed.

"Traffic's not bad for a Sunday," said Clovis as they left the Purley Way behind. "Very quiet."

"Aren't the verges and hedgerows pretty?" said Candy. "All the berries and flowers. Will you guys sit still! Dalai! Tangra Tso! Leave it alone. Oh, Clovis, they've ripped the wrapping paper to shreds. I'll have to take it off. I'm sorry. Do you think it will be all right with just the ribbon and the gift tag. Will it look tacky not to have wrapped it? It was meant to look so special."

"No, it'll be fine. Don't worry. She's going to love it."

She'd better after Candy had brought it back in a taxi from the Edgware Road. He anticipated Izzie's reaction on seeing it with mixed feelings.

Miranda Ingram, sitting on the front step with her arms round her knees, her face puffy with crying, heard the car before it turned the sharp corner to the drive. The two dogs tore off to meet it. She couldn't believe what she was hearing. How could they? How could they? Abba's "Dancing Queen" was blaring through the open windows as the car pulled up and there was Dad at the wheel and Lyris in the passenger seat. In the back was a woman in a big pink hat with dogs jumping and yapping all over her and sitting beside her, wearing a seatbelt, was the hugest, most hideous ceramic Dalmatian Miranda had ever seen, with a scarlet bow round its neck.

"Where is everybody? I thought we'd have to park in the paddock," said Clovis as he opened the car doors for Lyris and Candy. "We must be the first."

He took the flowers from the boot and saw Miranda walking slowly towards them. He waved, then broke into a run, taken by surprise by love as he was every time. He could feel his grin stretching seldom-used muscles in his face. Miranda ran at him, throwing her arms around him, knocking him off balance.

"Oh Dad, I'm so glad you've come. It's so terrible. I can't bear it."

"Darling, sweetheart, angel, what's so terrible? Tell me. I can put it right for you. Daddy's here now."

"You can't, how could you? Nobody can ever again."

He lifted her head and saw her swollen face, "Miranda, tell me! What's happened, for God's sake?"

"Haven't you heard? Don't you know? She's dead."

"Dead? Your mother's dead?"

"Princess Diana's dead. Diana's dead. In a car crash. And Dodi as well."

"I don't believe it. She can't be."

It flashed through his mind that Isobel had somehow engineered it to spoil her party. His legs weakened and he sat on the grass pulling Miranda with him. Clovis didn't know if he was crying for the princess, at Miranda's grief or in relief that Isobel wasn't dead.

Behind them Candy teetered on her heels trying to disentangle her dogs from the Ingram pair. The brim of her hat was bent, her skirt was creased to buggery and she could see it was going to be an action replay of the Carmody country disaster. Lyris, in black sprigged with colored flowers and a straw hat, was carrying the Dalmatian. Isobel came out of the house and sat on the grass beside Clovis. Candy saw that she was wearing jeans and an old jersey and her hair was frizzing out wildly from a cotton bandanna.

"Is it true?" Clovis asked Isobel.

Her tear-stained face confirmed the news, but she nodded before jumping up to take the slippery dog from Lyris who was staggering under its weight.

"Lyris, you shouldn't have. A card would have been quite enough. But thank you. He's frightfully amusing," she sobbed.

"Happy birthday, Izzie. This is Candy. The present is hers. I was just carrying it for her."

Lyris *had* thought a hand-painted card would have been enough. She began to fear that something was seriously wrong. Izzie looked as if she'd been crying for hours and she wasn't dressed for the party.

"Candy, I'm so sorry. How terrible of me. Thank you so much. He's adorable. And all your little dogs, such fun to have them all here." She wept into the Dalmatian's chest.

Talk about over-reacting, Candy thought, it's only a dog, even if it did cost an arm and a leg.

"Actually, it's from both of us. Clovis and me, I mean. Happy birthday, Isobel. Congratulations on attaining the Big Five Oh. Thank you so much for inviting me. It's lovely to meet you," she said.

"How can you stand there and congratulate me? Wishing me a happy birthday, how could you both? Have you no feelings at all?" Tears were rolling down her face.

Candy walked over to Clovis and Miranda. "Would somebody mind telling me what's going on? Has something happened?"

Isobel had been woken by a telephone call from her sister at six o'clock. She had managed to get hold of all the guests who had not rung her themselves, but she felt that Clovis should be there for Miranda's sake.

"Shall we have this off for a bit?" Clovis asked. "It's not as though they're going to announce that it's all been a dreadful mistake."

Izzie switched off the television.

"Now I understand why the Purseys' flower stall was doing such good business," said Lyris.

"I still can't believe we didn't know. It seems so awful somehow," Candy said, crying again. "Those poor poor little boys."

Clovis envied her her ability to express the emotions he felt but could not have articulated.

Miranda asked him, "Why aren't all the bells tolling?"

"They will. They will."

They were sitting in the kitchen drinking coffee and wine, picking at party food and feeding titbits to the seven dogs. A van from a charity in Sevenoaks was coming to pick up most of the food later. The birthday cake made by Miranda was on the table, stripped of its candles, with bare patches in the icing where she had removed the decorations. Clovis's flowers were standing, still in their paper, in an earthernware urn.

Candy said, "No wonder everything felt so weird this morning. London was in a state of shock."

" 'Brightness falls from the air; Queens have died young and fair . . .' " said Lryis.

Two friends of Miranda's, a girl and a boy, came to the back door, and when Miranda took them up to her room, they left behind them a sense of loss. "Don't go, we need you," Clovis wanted to call after them. Candy gazed after Miranda, poignantly tall and fair-haired, and reflected that Miranda was the age that she herself had been when she had left for London. It seemed to her in the silence left by the voices of Miranda's friends, fading and disappearing as they ascended the stairs, that Miranda had stepped into the future she wished had been hers.

Izzie clasped one of Candy's hands and one of Clovis's hands in her own.

"I'm so pleased that Clovis has you, Candy. We must all take great care of each other. I've been making plans for the future myself," she went on, releasing their hands. "I had thought that by being a magistrate I might be able to make a difference, now I'm not so sure. Often I find the burden of human suffering and cruelty too heavy to bear and for some time I considered applying to join a Contemplative Order, when Miranda is settled of course, where I could join my voice with those seeking to fight evil with the power of prayer. But then it came to me that I should establish my own Order. A sort of unofficially recognised community, a band of folk dedicated to living simply, dressing perhaps in some unobtrusive uniform, going about the world helping in little ways, righting wrongs by stealth."

"Like the Masons?" asked Clovis.

Candy had to bite an olive. She had pictured a gray hooded figure flitting into a hotel bathroom to replace with her own the towels that departing guests had stolen.

"Well, I'll make some more coffee, shall I?" said Isobel.

Lyris murmured to Clovis, "Everybody seems so determined to do good lately. Do you think it would be a refreshing change to meet someone avowed to doing something really *bad*?"

He winced.

CHAPTER TWENTY-FOUR

Lyris had come home from Isobel's party to find a note from Jacki saying she had gone to be with her parents. It was extraordinary to be feeling this personal grief, this pain at the fairytale gone rotten. She was relieved to be alone and yet the house felt empty even with the cats to greet her.

Jacki returned two days later carrying a pile of newspapers, two pairs of white overalls supplied by her father and a sheaf of shade cards which she'd picked out herself. Her eyes were red.

"I rang the Louis Viner Gallery from home. They said sales had been a bit disappointing up till now but somebody had bought number 34, the Romney Marsh, this morning. A Mr. Ingram. I wonder if it was your friend Mr. Ingram?"

"I wonder."

"I never knew how much I loved her," Jacki burst out. "I never imagined this could happen. Not to Diana. She was a bright star that shone for a while and now she's gone forever. Just when she might have found happiness at last. She had her troubles just like you and me but that only made her more . . . she truly was the People's Princess. Everything feels so weird. It's like history is happening and we're all part of it."

"I think we're in danger of genuine grief being whipped up

into something ugly," said Lyris. "Blow your nose and put those newspapers away and let's work out some color schemes."

Later she saw that a color portrait of Diana had been pinned to the back of the spare-room door. It seemed as if the whole country hung suspended in time.

Lyris and Jacki watched the funeral on television together. The days went on and still people laid bunches of flowers outside Kensington Palace and hung poems and toys on the trees until the park was a sea of cellophane flashing in the sun that glittered off a thousand scarlet and crimson hearts.

The Lees' son Russell had agreed to paint the outside doors and window frames, and replace any which had rotted. Lyris decided that she and Jacki should make a start on the front room.

"These overalls are hilarious. We look like a couple of clowns," said Jacki when they first put them on.

"I think you look rather fetching in yours," Lyris told her.

Lyris wanted to get the work done as quickly as possible because she felt what she recognized as an irrational guilt about changing the way the house had looked when John lived there. Jacki proved an enthusiastic shifter of furniture and stripper of walls and woodwork. Like a true professional she placed a blaring little radio on the floor.

Perhaps this is where her talent lies, Lyris thought, watching her applying undercoat as she rested in a dust-sheet draped chair. Jacki was wearing a baseball cap while Lyris's own white hair was spattered with whiter paint. A pale moth butted the glass of the open window. It was ten o'clock in the evening and growing dark, the streetlights were on but Jacki had one wall to finish.

"That's it then," she said, wiping her hands on her hips. "I'd better just close the window."

She leaned out over the sill to breathe the night air, and pulled her head back in as if she'd been bitten.

"It's Nathan! Nathan's coming up the road!"

Nathan stood still on the pavement. The effect of the drink he'd had to fortify himself had worn off leaving a sick feeling of fear. He was about to turn back when a tall white figure emerged from Lyris's gate, looked down the street and saw him, and then Lyris was walking, striding along the pavement, loping towards him like an arctic hare.

COLOPHON

Shena Mackay was born in Scotland and published her first novel at the age of 20. She is the editor of *Such Devoted Sisters*, and author of four novels, *An Advent Calendar, A Bowl of Cherries, Dunedin,* and *The Orchard on Fire* and a collection of short stories, *Dreams of Dead Women's Handbags*. She lives in London.

The text was composed by Alabama Book Composition, Deatsville, Alabama. The text typeface is Bembo with display faces of Bremen and Bembo.

The book was printed by Data Reproductions of Auburn Hills, Michigan on elemental chlorine and acid-free recycled paper with soy-based ink.